On the Island

Iain Crichton Smith was born on 1 January 1928 on the island of Lewis and was educated in Stornoway and at the University of Aberdeen.

Until 1977, when he became a full-time writer, he was a teacher in Clydebank and Oban. He has won several literary prizes and was made an OBE in 1980.

IAIN CRICHTON SMITH

On the Island

**With drawings by
Carol Fowke**

Richard Drew Publishing
Glasgow

First published by
Victor Gollancz Limited 1979

This edition first published 1988 by

Richard Drew Publishing Limited
6 Clairmont Gardens, Glasgow G3 7LW
Scotland

The publisher acknowledges the financial assistance of the
Scottish Arts Council in the publication of this book.

British Library Cataloguing in Publication Data

Smith, Iain Crichton, *1928 —*
    On the island
    I. Title II. Fowke, carol
    823'.914[J]

    ISBN 0-86267-226-0

Printed and bound in Great Britain by
Cox & Wyman Ltd., Reading

1

IAIN SAT ON the pier swinging his legs and looking down into the water. There was an iron ladder, slimy with seaweed, set into the stone and he had always wanted to climb down it, but was afraid of doing so. In his nostrils there was the tart smell of brine, and his brown jersey stirred slightly in the sea breeze. He looked over at a rock on which a seagull was perched, turning its head from side to side as if it was studying the sea like a human being and thinking deeply.

I must climb down the ladder today, Iain was thinking, but there was no one there but himself and he was frightened of falling into the sea and drowning, for he couldn't swim. Really he shouldn't have been there at all, for it was Sunday, and all the houses were lying in a deep slumber; but he thought that if he actually wasn't doing anything, such as swimming, it would be all right for him to be there. Maybe, he thought, climbing down the ladder might be considered "doing something", and because he was frightened he thought that might be the case. Perhaps he should leave it till a weekday.

The sun beat on the water, and made it a wide trembling glitter as far as he could see. He noticed that the sea near the land was green, but that further out it became blue. He left the pier and went to the back of it, clambering among the rocks and gazing down into the pools. He was looking for crabs but he couldn't see any. The water in most of the pools was a soupy green, as if it were full of vegetables. He scrambled among the rocks finding here and there old wooden boxes, damp and broken, which had been

washed in on the waves, and lots of cardboard which perhaps the sailors threw overboard. Once he found a doll with no head and only one red chubby leg, and another time a decayed seagull which had only a few feathers left. He sat on a rock and looked out at the island which was set in the bay and on which sheep grazed, and wished that he could go over to it, but there was no way of doing so. The island was long and green and beyond it on the far horizon he could see ships sailing.

The silence around him apart from the heaving of the sea was profound. It was the silence of Sunday which was the greatest silence there was, and even when he looked back to the village he could see nothing moving on the road, not a person, not a car. The houses seemed to have withdrawn like crabs into the earth itself. The silence entered his head and sat there as if on a salty rock.

"I am Silence," it said.

Silence had a small black head like a gull's head.

The sea swayed all round him, sighing gently as if it were sad. Mixed with the smell of brine there was a scent of rank flowers, some of them red, which he saw growing along the top of the shore and above the dry cracked boats.

Iain liked the sea, for it told him stories. It told him of Spanish galleons, and Nelson's ships, and great liners, and little fishing boats. It told him of ships with masts and rigging and boys with buckled shoes. It told him of whales and sharks and herring and mackerel and dogfish and cod. It sang in his head, and it seemed to course through his body as naturally as blood. He liked to watch the waves running to the shore, collapsing, and threading inwards on the sand, as thin as spittle.

He went down to the sand from the pier and felt it hot to his touch. He lay on it looking up at the sky, where the clouds passed slowly by, high and white. As he gazed it seemed as if it was the earth itself that was moving, just as when one looked down into the water from the pier it seemed after a while as if it was the pier that was moving. He felt the heat of the sun on his brow and on his knees and on the part of his throat that was exposed above the jersey. Above him he saw a seagull flying and for a moment he looked directly into its dull eye which knew nothing of humanity.

Under the heat of the sun he felt as if he was going to fall asleep, but at the same time he knew that he should be home soon, for his mother would be waiting for him. How nice it was to be alone and not fighting with his brother, Kenneth. How pleasant it was to be completely alone beside the sea, and feeling the heat of the sun on his body. A wasp buzzed round him and he scratched his head.

The sea was singing its song in his head. It was filling it with all sorts of stories, chests with treasure in them, pirates in black coats,

7

skull and crossbones flying bravely in the slight breeze. The pirates were waving cutlasses which flashed like new moons. They swore fearfully below their flags. They were rushing towards him, their swords becoming heavier and heavier and heavier. Then they finally faded away into the darkness.

Iain slept.

When he woke up, the day seemed to have turned slightly dark, and Iain looked around him in fear, for the sea itself had a dark shade running along it like a bruise, as had the grass which was waving in a stronger breeze. The rocks stood out of the water, cold and dark and apparently more distant than they had been before. The island, long and dark, had lost its greenness. Suddenly Iain got to his feet and ran, away from the dry beached boats, from the rocks, from the pier, from the cooling sand, and his feet flashed along a road which too had turned dark.

All the time he was running he didn't see anybody: it was as if there was no one alive in the whole world, as if the silence had become threatening and empty. He pushed open the iron gate at the end of the road and ran faster than ever, though now there was a stitch in his side. He climbed over the grassy wall to the path which lay between the cornfields in which red flowers were growing and whose strong scent he could feel in his nostrils.

His feet seemed to be drumming out the words, Everyone's gone. I am alone. The wetness of the grass seeped into his shoes. He was climbing a brae along the path which had been beaten by the many feet of the villagers, both in time past and in the present, as they had made their way to the well which was hidden, like a cool mouth, among tall grass. He followed the path till he came to the first house, which was silent behind its tangled garden, crouched into the earth. And still he had seen no one, no car, no bicycle. Sunday hung over the whole world: there was even no smoke from any of the houses.

Then off to his left he saw a cow deep in grass. The cow was brown and its head was buried in the grass and its tail was flicking flies away from its body. Suddenly it raised its large heavy head and looked ruminatively at him, with its big stupid eyes. Carefully Iain went up to it and he saw that its eyes were tearful, for the flies were buzzing inside them and about the bony head, humming blackly and busily in the day. The cow gazed helplessly back at him with its large liquid eyes, its tail swishing backwards and forwards like a pendulum. Slowly Iain put out his hand and patted the hard head, while the eyes gazed at him mournfully and sadly.

After a while he turned away, walking slowly to his own house, over the flowers which were growing from the beaten earth, and stepping very carefully between them lest he should kill any of them. He walked across the plank and up the path to his house. He waited a while at the door, for the house was as silent as the others. Then he opened the door and ran into the living room where his mother was sitting in a chair reading the Bible. She turned and looked at him, through her large spectacles which she only wore on Sunday.

"Where have you been?" she asked.

Iain looked at her, at the clock on the mantelpiece, at the bed on one side of the room, at the sideboard with the dishes on it, and said, "I don't know."

2

ONE DAY WHEN Iain was sitting in class looking at Miss Stilton and thinking that she was as thin as a pencil – though he was frightened of her too – he saw a boy wearing his clothes sitting at a desk in front of the teacher. The boy was wearing Iain's own green stockings, green jersey and green woollen shorts. All through the lesson he watched him and he was quite sure that it was his clothes he was wearing, for only his mother made clothes like that. It was very odd seeing someone else in his clothes as if he were looking into a mirror – though the boy, whose name was Dan and who was the son of a tinker, wasn't like Iain at all, for Iain was pale and this boy was short and freckled. Iain was so surprised that even in the middle of the class he would have gone to speak to him if Miss Stilton hadn't been asking them questions. However, they were doing English and Iain knew that Miss Stilton didn't want to be interrupted, especially at English, for she was very keen on spelling and parts of speech. He looked down at his own green clothes and then across at Dan in his dress of reflected green.

Miss Stilton was asking Dan what a noun was and Dan was half standing half sitting in his seat, his mouth opening and shutting. "Don't you know what a noun is, boy?" Miss Stilton repeated, tapping the desk with her pointer. "I thought I told everybody what a noun was. Everybody else knows what a noun is. How do you not know? Do you think I am going to stand here day after day asking you questions about what a noun is when you don't bother to listen to anything that I say? Why do you think I write these things down on a blackboard? Eh? Are you deaf or blind or what?'' And she banged the desk with the pointer while the class sat up petrified in their seats.

Dan half sat and half stood awkwardly in his seat, and he looked funny and frightened. Iain gazed at Miss Stilton and thought how he might kill her. First of all he thought of putting her in a pot and having savages dancing round her waving spears. There would be drums beating and there would be feathers shaking and there would be birds of bright tropical colours with big long beaks clacking from the branches. After that he thought he would stretch her on a rack till her legs extended so far that they would go over the horizon. Then he thought he would lay her head on a block and have an executioner with a black mask cut it off.

Dan was very frightened and his freckled face was flushed with nervousness. For some reason there was spittle coming out of his mouth and Iain watched it with fascination. It seemed to him – because of the clothes Dan was wearing – that it was himself who was being attacked by Miss Stilton, though he thought that he wouldn't have allowed spittle to spoil the neatness of his jersey. Miss Stilton banged on the desk again and told Dan to sit down. "Next time," she said, "you will know what a noun is or I will know the reason why. What is a noun?" she asked the class and they all chorused, "A noun is the name of an object, miss." A jersey was a noun, Iain thought, shorts was a noun, green, however, was an adjective. The desk was a noun, but a desk was also varnished and had a smell. And smell was a noun. Or was it. Was Miss Stilton a noun? The light poured in through the window and showed him clearly the green clothes that he might have been wearing himself.

When the bell went he accosted Dan during the interval, where he was standing beside the tap in the playground. He had a firm intention of asking him where he had got his clothes from, but when he saw him, alone and miserable, he decided that he wouldn't question him at all. Maybe it was a miracle. Maybe they weren't his clothes after all.

"Have you any marbles?" he asked Dan.

Dan looked at him and said that he hadn't. He seemed even more suspicious and distant than usual. Iain thought of giving him some, but decided that he wouldn't, since he had enough of his property already.

"Do you live in a tent?" he asked seriously.

"Yes. What's that to you," Dan replied, bristling as if he was going to attack him.

"I was only asking. Is it cold?"

"No, it's not."

"Do you have dogs?"

"Yes."

"Do you travel all over then?"

"Yes."

"Have you been to Spain?"

"Yes."

"Have you been to Czechoslovakia?"

"Yes."

Iain tried a last thrust. "Have you been to Paraguay?"

"Yes."

But Iain knew he hadn't been to Paraguay. He might have been to Spain and Czechoslovakia, but not to Paraguay. Paraguay was in South America.

Suddenly Dan said, "I can drink more water than you." And he bent his head with its carrot-colour hair under the tap and began to drink, letting the water slorp down his throat.

"The water is going on your jersey," said Iain suddenly. "You're dirtying your jersey."

"Shut up," said Dan and pulled away from the tap.

"I can drink more water than you," said Iain and he also began to drink, feeling that he was being choked by the flood of cold water which poured down his throat. Finally, gasping, he drew his head away, knowing that Dan had won.

"I'll tell you something," he said," You haven't as many stamps as me."

"I don't like stamps," said Dan. Then Iain noticed that his jersey had been patched at the front and the wool used was a different colour from the rest. It wasn't green at all, it was a dark brown. It was like seeing a field, part of which had been burnt. Also there was a smell coming from Dan, the smell of someone who hasn't had a bath for a long time. Iain tried to imagine what Dan's mother was like. He thought of her as having a brown face like a nut and carrying a string of cans over her shoulder, and sitting by her tent eating turnips and carrots which she had stolen from the fields.

"It's all right," he said," You can have one of my stamps. Do you want one?"

"No," said Dan. "I don't want any of your old stamps. I've got stamps at home." And he ran away shouting and Iain ran after him.

"Hey," he said. "Come back, come back. You can have my jersey." But Dan didn't seem to hear him and he cannoned into Miss Stilton, who was coming round the corner of the old stone building in her black suit.

Iain stopped dead a few feet away while Dan stood staring up at Miss Stilton. A smile came over Miss Stilton's face and it was a beautiful smile, it was a slow lovely smile, and then she said to Dan," I'll see you in my room after the interval." And she passed on, still smiling, till she entered the school by the big main door, the pupils making way for her as she walked.

Dan started to cry and Iain went up to him. "I'll tell you what to do,' he said. "I'll take off my scarf and you can put it next to your. . ." – he hesitated – "bum. . . . It won't hurt you then."

"That's no good," said Dan tearfully, "She hits you on the hand." Iain had forgotten this, for he read a lot of stories about public schools where a cane was used, and in any case he himself had never been beaten in school.

"I'd forgotten," he said. "I could go instead of you but she would know me." He was thinking that perhaps Miss Stilton might not tell them apart in their green clothes. He really had no intention of going in place of Dan but he wanted Dan to think well of him, to consider him a hero.

"That's daft," said Dan.

Iain shook Dan by the hand very seriously and said, "It won't last. You'll see." And then without thinking he added, "I'm sorry about the patch."

"What are you talking about?" said Dan.

"Nothing. Nothing. I hope she dies. I hope she drops dead. And I hope the vultures eat her."

Iain watched Dan go into Miss Stilton's room after the interval and he was glad that it wasn't him, for in his imagination he could feel her belt with two black thongs bite into his hand. He was glad in a way that it was Dan who had to go, though he didn't dislike him.

When Dan came out of her room, his mouth was twisted in pain, his hands rubbing against his green jersey, Iain's green jersey. Iain ran up to him and said, "I'm sorry. Was it sore?"

"Oh, shut up," said Dan. "Go away."

That night Iain told his mother about the green suit and she told him that Dan's mother had come round the houses one day looking for rags and she had given her Iain's old green suit which he had outgrown.

"You shouldn't have," said Iain. "Tinkers are very ungrateful. They don't care. Anyway I nearly punched him today."

"Punched him," said Kenneth, his younger brother, and laughed.

"Well, I nearly did," said Iain. "He's getting too big for his boots. And he smells. And he tells lies as well."

3

ONE WINTER'S DAY Iain and his younger brother Kenneth had another of their fights. It happened in the attic which they used to get into by climbing up the inside of the main door and then swinging themselves on to the floor above. This particular day, Kenneth began to swing to and fro like a pendulum from one of the rafters while below him, sitting on a box, Iain was reading an old copy of the *Chambers Journal* which he had found in an ancient trunk. The *Chambers Journal* had double columns of very small writing in old-fashioned stately language which appealed to Iain, as well as drawings of gentlemen and ladies in odd dresses. Iain was quite happy sitting there while Kenneth swung on the rafters, turning upside down and looking at him as if he were an ape on a tree.

Kenneth was smaller than Iain but stronger and more athletic: he had climbed down the iron stairs at the pier dozens of times and he had even climbed the roof of the house by means of a ladder when it was being tarred. He had stood on top of the chimney head crowing like a cockerel in his red jersey.

His feet touched Iain's head on one of his swings.

"Stop that," said Iain in an irritated voice.

"What?" said Kenneth innocently, upside down and gazing down at him.

"Hitting my head," said Iain. "Can't you see that I'm reading?"

"I can't help it," said Kenneth still swinging.

"Well, stop swinging then," said Iain.

"I like swinging," said Kenneth. "Why don't you swing?"

"I'm reading."

"Well, move away then."

"I told you I'm reading. Why should I move away? You stop swinging."

"I can't swing anywhere but here, can I?"

"You can stop. . . ."

"No," said Kenneth and he hit Iain on the head again with his feet.

Iain thought Kenneth was being unreasonable and so they had a fight, and they rolled backwards and forwards till Kenneth finally pinned Iain down on the floor, face upwards.

"Surrender?" he said breathlessly. "Surrender?"

"No," said Iain, so Kenneth pressed his knee into his stomach.

"Surrender," he said, growing more and more angry, and his face becoming redder and redder as if it would burst.

"No," said Iain again. So Kenneth got even angrier and his eyes grew wild and ferocious and he was about to butt Iain in the face till Iain said, "All right. I surrender."

Kenneth got to his feet again and began to swing on the rafter as if nothing had happened, and Iain was left alone. I could kill him, he thought, I could kick his face in. And he imagined himself as an officer giving orders that Kenneth should be taken to a small room and tortured with a needle through his head.

Outside it was very windy and it was growing dark again. When he went over to the skylight he could see the grass moving restlessly as it did in a storm. There was no rain as yet, only the strong wind. It was about five o'clock. He saw some hens being blown about in their brown skirts and then he saw Tonkan standing at the fence spitting into his hands, before he started work with a hammer on one of the posts.

I hope he dies, he said to himself, I hope he dies, thinking of Kenneth. He imagined Kenneth holding his hand out from a tempestuous sea and himself on a boat and not helping him and

watching him drown. He thought of Kenneth leaving his last footprints on a snowy bridge as in a poem that he had read at school and which had made him cry though he wouldn't let Miss Stilton see him.

He tried to read his book again but found that he couldn't because his mind wasn't on it and the room was growing so dark that he couldn't make out the small writing. There was a storm rising, he could feel it in his bones, and through the window he could see the grey leaden waves and the boats pitching stumpily like tubs. He wanted it to be a really big storm, a terrible storm, so that the rain would pour down and there would be wind, lightning and thunder, and the world would be full of water and he himself would be up in the attic as if he was a Noah watching everything and he would be safe.

But after a while he grew tired of watching Kenneth swinging and he climbed down the door again and went into the kitchen. His mother was baking and she said, "Where's Kenneth?" At that moment he heard the door closing and he knew that Kenneth had also climbed down the door and had gone out.

"I don't know," he said

"How do you mean, 'I don't know'? I thought he was in the attic."

"He's not. He went out." He wondered if he could get a scone, but didn't dare to ask for one. If Kenneth wanted to go out in the storm that was his lookout.

"Well, has he gone out then?"

"I think so."

His mother stopped what she was doing and looked at him. "Do you hear that wind?" she said. "It's going to be a storm," and her voice trembled. "Where's that boy gone to? I hope he hasn't gone down to the sea again."

Suddenly there was a clap of thunder which seemed to run along the roof like someone with heavy boots banging it and then there was a stab of lightning which lighted up the scones.

"Oh," screamed his mother. "Get cloths. Cloths from somewhere. Don't just stand there."

"Cloths?" he said, standing there stupidly. "Cloths? What cloths?"

"Oh, I'll get them," she said, her voice still high and trembling. And she ran over to the dresser and began to drag out sheets. She began to cover the mirrors with them, the one that was hanging on the wall and the one on the dresser itself.

"Don't you know," she said in the same high voice, "that you must cover the mirrors when there is lightning. Lightning can get in but sometimes it can't get out."

Her voice was rising and falling like the wind itself. "Where's that boy gone to?"

Iain was standing in the middle of the floor not knowing what to do. Through the window he could see the fences swaying and bending in the wind and the rain lashing the ditches and bouncing from the earth and the plank that was at the foot of the path. Seagulls seemed to be held in perfect motionlessness by the wind. Suddenly there was another flash of lightning like teeth opening and he thought of Kenneth out in the storm drenched to the skin, the lightning knifing him and the thunder bouncing off him like a big football.

And he began to cry.

"I hope he'll be all right," he chanted monotonously. "I hope he'll be all right." And he rushed over to his mother and said, "I think Kenneth is going to die. What are we going to do?" And he remembered how Kenneth had given him a piece of chocolate one day and another time when he had saved him from a hiding from Crusty.

The rain was lashing down, the wind was blowing everything about and it was growing dark, and Iain saw in his mind's eye Kenneth struggling along, his mouth opening and shutting in the gusts of wind, and he thought that Kenneth was making his will to himself, and asking God's forgiveness for what he had done to Iain. "Please God," he imagined Kenneth saying, "forgive me. I'm sorry about Iain. I won't do it again. I won't swing from the rafter again and hit him with my feet. I won't try to butt his face again."

Kenneth's body as if burnt by the lightning was swinging on the rafter like that of a hanged man, and now and again Iain could see one eye glaring at him and asking for mercy. Kenneth's clothes had been drenched by the rain and his feet hung straight down.

"I'm going to look for him," he said.

"No," shrieked his mother. And she grabbed him. "You stay here and stop your nonsense."

But Iain was now thinking of Kenneth cowering in a cave, and himself riding up on his white horse and standing there in the lightning and the rain, and the horse neighing and shaking its head, and himself hauling Kenneth up behind him.

"Don't worry," he was saying over and over. "It will be all right. You're safe now. The White Knight has got you. The White Knight never fails." And the two of them rode on through the rain and lightning and thunder, as to all sides of them illuminated stage coaches rocked and swayed and Iain could see frightened faces at the windows and people pulling their hats down lest they should be blinded by the lightning.

"I'm going to get Kenneth," he shouted to his mother. "It was all my fault." And his mother hung on to him and the lightning flashed and stabbed at the walls of the room, and her eyes were shut, and her face was white with fear.

And then quite suddenly there was an enormous silence. And the two of them stood there in the middle of the silence. His mother's eyes slowly opened and she looked around her. The floor of the room steadied. The rain stopped pouring and racing. There was one last fading peal of thunder and then the silence returned, this time absolutely. They stood facing each other across the table with the warm scones between them. The white shrouds still draped the mirrors as if they were concealing dead people. As if in a dream his mother went over and pulled the cloths away, but she did not look in the mirrors.

Iain stood there amazed, almost falling to his knees in the quietness. He turned and looked through the window and saw that the insane jigsaw of road and ditch and grass had come to rest. A horse was standing by a stone wall drenched and passive after the rain, its head drooping. There was even a little wavering sunlight.

Then out of the calm they heard running footsteps and there was Kenneth rushing through the doorway and standing in front of them. He was perfectly dry as if he had been in some other house all the time.

"You bad boy," his mother shrieked at him, "You bad wicked boy," and she began to hit him so that Kenneth had to run all round the table and between the chairs. "You bad wicked boy," and she hit him again and again when she could catch him. And Iain watched the two of them till finally his mother gave up and Kenneth was crying. He was so happy to see Kenneth being punished, it was better for him than to be dead.

4

"I'LL TELL YOU something," said Daial to Iain. "I believe in ghosts."

It was Hallowe'en night and they were sitting in Daial's house—which was a thatched one—eating apples and cracking nuts which they had got earlier that evening from the people of the village. It was frosty outside and the night was very calm.

"I don't believe in ghosts," said Iain, munching an apple. "You've never seen a ghost, have you?"

"No," said Daial fiercely, "but I know people who have. My father saw a ghost at the Corner. It was a woman in a white dress."

"I don't believe it," said Iain. "It was more likely a piece of paper." And he laughed out loud. "It was more likely a newspaper. It was the local newspaper."

"I tell you he did," said Daial. "And another thing. They say that if you look between the ears of a horse you will see a ghost. I was told that by my granny."

"Horses' ears," said Iain laughing, munching his juicy apple. "Horses' ears."

Outside it was very very still, the night was, as it were, entranced under the stars.

"Come on then," said Daial urgently, as if he had been angered by Iain's dismissive comments. "We can go and see now. It's eleven o'clock and if there are any ghosts you might see them now. I dare you."

"All right," said Iain, throwing the remains of the apple into the fire. "Come on then."

And the two of them left the house, shutting the door carefully and noiselessly behind them and entering the calm night with its millions of stars. They could feel their shoes creaking among the frost, and there were little panes of ice on the small pools of water on the road. Daial looked very determined, his chin thrust out as if his honour had been attacked. Iain liked Daial fairly well though Daial hardly read any books and was only interested in fishing and football. Now and again as he walked along he looked up at the sky with its vast city of stars and felt almost dizzy because of its immensity.

"That's the Plough there," said Iain, "do you see it? Up there."

"Who told you that?" said Daial.

"I saw a picture of it in a book. It's shaped like a plough."

"It's not at all," said Daial. "It's not shaped like a plough at all. You never saw a plough like that in your life."

They were gradually leaving the village now, had in fact passed the last house, and Iain in spite of his earlier protestations was getting a little frightened, for he had heard stories of ghosts at the Corner before. There was one about a sailor home from the Merchant Navy who was supposed to have seen a ghost and after he had rejoined his ship he had fallen from a mast to the deck and had died instantly. People in the village mostly believed in ghosts. They believed that some people had the second sight and could see in advance the body of someone who was about to die though at that particular time he might be walking among them, looking perfectly healthy.

Daial and Iain walked on through the ghostly whiteness of the frost and it seemed to them that the night had turned much colder and also more threatening. There was no noise even of flowing water, for all the streams were locked in frost.

"It's here they see the ghosts," said Daial in a whisper, his voice trembling a little, perhaps partly with the cold. "If we had a horse we might see one."

"Yes," said Iain still trying to joke, though at the same time he also found himself whispering. "You could ride the horse and look between its ears."

The whole earth was a frosty globe, creaking and spectral, and the shine from it was eerie and faint.

"Can you hear anything?" said Daial who was keeping close to Iain.

"No," said Iain. "I can't hear anything. There's nothing. We should go back."

"No," Daial replied, his teeth chattering. "W-w-e w-w-on't go back. We have to stay for a while."

"What would you do if you saw a ghost?" said Iain.

"I would run," said Daial, "I would run like hell."

"I don't know what I would do," said Iain, and his words seemed to echo through the silent night. "I might drop dead. Or I might . . ." He suddenly had a terrible thought. Perhaps they were ghosts themselves and the ghost who looked like a ghost to them might be a human being after all. What if a ghost came towards them and then walked through them smiling, and then they suddenly realised that they themselves were ghosts.

"Hey, Daial," he said, "what if we are . . ." And then he stopped, for it seemed to him that Daial had turned all white in the frost, that his head and the rest of his body were white, and his legs and shoes were also a shining white. Daial was coming towards him with his mouth open, and where there had been a head there was only a bony skull, its interstices filled with snow. Daial was walking towards him, his hands outstretched, and they were bony without any skin on them. Daial was his enemy, he was a ghost who wished to destroy him, and that was why he had led him out to the Corner to the territory of the ghosts. Daial was not Daial at all, the real Daial was back in the house, and this was a ghost that had taken over Daial's body in order to entice Iain to the place where he was now. Daial was a devil, a corpse.

And suddenly Iain began to run and Daial was running after him. Iain ran crazily with frantic speed but Daial was close on his heels. He was running after him and his white body was blazing with the frost and it seemed to Iain that he was stretching his bony arms towards him. They raced along the cold white road which was so hard that their shoes left no prints on it, and Iain's heart was beating like a hammer, and then they were in the village among the ordinary lights and now they were at Daial's door.

"What happened," said Daial panting, leaning against the door, his breath coming in huge gasps.

And Iain knew at that moment that this really was Daial, whatever had happened to the other one, and that this one would think of him as a coward for the rest of his life and tell his pals how Iain had run away. And he was even more frightened than he had been before, till he knew what he had to do.

"I saw it," he said.

"What?" said Daial, his eyes growing round with excitement.

"I saw it," said Iain again. "Didn't you see it?"

"What?" said Daial." What did you see?"

"I saw it," said Iain, "but maybe you don't believe me."

"What did you see?" said Daial. "I believe you."

"It was a coffin," said Iain. "I saw a funeral."

"A funeral?"

"I saw a funeral," said Iain, "and there were people in black hats and black coats. You know?"

Daial nodded eagerly.

"And I saw them carrying a coffin," said Iain,"and it was all yellow, and it was coming straight for you. You didn't see it. I know you didn't see it. And I saw the coffin open and I saw the face in the coffin."

"The face?" said Daial and his eyes were fixed on Iain's face, and Iain could hardly hear what he was saying.

"And do you know whose face it was?"

"No," said Daial breathlessly. "Whose face was it? Tell me, tell me."

"It was your face," said Iain in a high voice. "It was your face."

Daial paled.

"But it's all right," said Iain. "I saved you. If the coffin doesn't touch you you're all right. I read that in a book. That's why I ran. I knew that you would run after me. And you did. And I saved you. For the coffin would have touched you if I hadn't run."

"Are you sure," said Daial, in a frightened trembling voice. "Are you sure that I'm saved?"

"Yes," said Iain. "I saw the edge of the coffin and it was almost touching the patch on your trousers and then I ran."

"Gosh," said Daial, "that's something. You must have the second sight. It almost touched me. Gosh. Wait till I tell the boys tomorrow. You wait." And then as if it had just occurred to him he said, "You believe in ghosts now, don't you?"

"Yes, I believe, " said Iain.

"There you are then," said Daial. "Gosh. Are you sure if they don't touch you you're all right."

"Cross my heart," said Iain.

5

IT WAS WINTER time and the snow was billowing round the cottage where Iain stayed with Kenneth and his mother, and the glittering light was almost dazzling. So attracted was Iain by the waves of snow and the light that he put on his wellingtons and went outside.

In front of him and around him he could see the houses of the village, with snow on their roofs and doors, as if they existed in a fairy tale. Blue smoke rose vaguely from the chimneys and was dissipated in the still air. In his wellingtons he sank deep into the snow, finding no road anywhere and once sinking deep into a ditch, but though for a while he was frightened by this, his main feeling was intense joy to see the world so white and clear and sparkling, so that he wanted to burst out singing. The houses were like ships rising out of an ocean of snow, and on the telegraph wires, themselves covered with snow, he saw little birds perched as if they were clutching their little wings about them for warmth. It was a magical world, its purity was overwhelming: it was as if some being had calmly in the night rid the whole world of its detail – roads, tin cans, planks – so that all that was visible was an undulating sea of snow, more solid – seeming than an ordinary sea, but almost as treacherous.

Plunging his wellingtons into the snow, Iain plodded on, just for the sake of the walking and not because he was going anywhere in particular. Sometimes he felt that he was losing his balance and that he would keel over like an overloaded ship into the waves of white. When he turned and faced the moor all he could see was uninterrupted mounds of snow, rising and falling like a ghostly Atlantic. The world had been made anew under a blue sky: in the secrecy of the night it had been totally transformed. And into this new world Iain plodded.

He passed Big Norman's house which was sunk into the snow and saw like a ghost at the window Big Norman's wife peering out, as if surprised to see him there in the middle of the hillock of snow. She was still wearing her nightgown and Iain burst out laughing inside himself because he had caught her like that on that morning of whiteness.   He passed the house of Mrs Murray — whose husband was dead and who lived with her two teenage daughters, and who had a bad limp from her youth, and he heard as he crossed the snow music coming from the wireless. But this time he didn't see anyone at the window. The music floated over the wastes of snow, light and Christmasy. House after house he passed, his wellingtons sinking deep into the snow so that sometimes he was afraid that they would come off altogether and he would have to walk in his stocking soles. Once coming from somewhere out of the distant mounds of snow he heard a cock crowing cock-a-doodle-doo, and the strong notes pierced the calm day with absolute and regal clarity.

He was making his way slowly to the far end of the village and it was there he saw his first human being out in the snow. It was in fact Blinder who was kneeling down by the open door of a now totally white shed trying to get wood for his fire. He was called Blinder because he was blind, and this had happened as a result of two separate accidents. In the first one he had been playing with another boy at gouging out eyes and the other boy had, though not deliberately, gouged out his left eye. He had lost the second one when he had been out in a boat and an oar had gone into it. Nevertheless in spite of his blindness he had been known to climb on to the roof of his house and repair the aerial of the wireless, and was totally competent in the house where he lived alone.

"Hullo," Iain shouted to him and Blinder turned to him, the sticks in his hands, and Iain could have sworn that he was seeing him, so direct was his gaze.

"Hullo Iain," said Blinder, "it's a cold one."

"It's a cold one right enough," said Iain in his adult voice. It didn't occur to him to ask Blinder if he could help him with the sticks for he knew that Blinder wouldn't want that.

"Would you like to help me with the sticks?" said Blinder.

"All right," said Iain, for it was all right if Blinder asked first.

"They're full of snow," said Iain.

"You're right," said Blinder, "it will take a long time for them to thaw out."

They collected some sticks and then Blinder shut the shed door and locked it and they went into the house. Blinder laid the sticks by the fire to dry and Iain sat on the bench watching the merry light of the fire, and sometimes stretching out his hands in front of him to warm them.

"It's a great day though," he said.

"Yes," said Blinder. "I can feel it. It's very fresh."

As Iain watched him he poured tea into a teapot and then said: "Would you like a cup of tea?"

"All right," said Iain. "I'll take a cup." And he took the cup from Blinder and they sat there drinking tea together. The house was very tidy and the bed had already been made, for it was in the kitchen, and Iain could see it quite clearly. He noticed that the clock wasn't working.

"Well, Iain," said Blinder genially. "I haven't seen you for a long time. And what's your news?" His eyes turned towards Iain as if he were searching him for news, while he sat there just like anybody else with the cup of tea in his hand.

"I haven't any news," said Iain. "I don't think anything is happening." In spite of the fire his knees felt cold.

"That's right," said Blinder who seemed to be pleased that

nothing was happening. "Here, I'll show you something." And he walked over to a basket which was lying in a corner of the room.

"I found a bird," he said. "What bird is it?"

"I don't know," said Iain.

Then he looked more closely and he thought it might be a redbreast.

"I think it is a redbreast," he said.

"I thought it might be," said Blinder.

The bird was lying on its side in the basket and Blinder took it very gently in his hand while its beak feebly pecked. The beady eye of the bird looked at Iain with a blurred fierceness and it twisted a little in Blinder's large gentle hand.

"I think its wing is broken," said Blinder. "Can you see if it is?"

"I think it is," said Iain, bending down to look more closely. "What are you going to do?"

"I've been giving it hot milk, " said Blinder, "and I've been trying to splint its wing. I hope it won't die."

"I don't think so," said Iain as the bird began to flutter its one good wing while its little breast beat spasmodically and it stared at Iain with its beady eye.

"I'll put it back," said Blinder. "The warmth will help it."

"Yes," said Iain, "I'm sure it will."

They sat in silence for a little while and then Blinder said, "Have you any idea what the time is?"

"I don't know," said Iain, "it might be about eleven o'clock."

"I bet that everything is white," said Blinder. "I bet it's very white, isn't it?"

"Yes," said Iain, "it's very white and the snow is very deep and the sun is flashing off it. Only my wellingtons sink in it." It occurred to him that he was finding it difficult to describe to Blinder what the snow was really like, the billowing mounds of it, the intense sparkle, the newness of it. These were things that you couldn't easily tell anyone.

30

"That would be right," said Blinder putting his empty cup on the table. "I bet you it's white. I can feel it."

"Can you see anything at all?" said Iain in a little burst of words, as if he were asking something that should not be asked, and he therefore felt nervous like the little bird whose heart had beaten so spasmodically in the basket.

"No," said Blinder, "nothing at all. I can't see you at all. But I know your voice."

"It must be funny to be blind," said Iain. "I mean. . ."

"I can manage all right though," said Blinder. "I know where you are though I can't see you. It's not all that funny. I can't explain it."

"I bet you could find your way about the village better than me in the dark though," said Iain.

"That's right," said Blinder, "I could."

"I might fall into a well if it was dark," said Iain and he shuddered as he imagined himself falling and falling and shouting out of the dark water while the silence grew deeper and deeper around him.

"You could do that," said Blinder. "Do you want to go for a walk?"

"Yes." said Iain, "I wouldn't mind."

And they went out into the white glare again, and they walked through the snow, sinking into it, while now and again Iain heard the same or a different cock crow, and the houses were white with snow and the roofs were covered with it. Even the sky seemed bluer and more dazzling than usual.

"Take my hand," said Blinder, "if you like. I know what I'm doing. I know where the ditch is."

"All right," said Iain and he took Blinder's hand, feeling quite secure as he walked beside him through the deep waves of snow.

"Over there," said Blinder, "is the quarry. I bet you can't see it, can you?"

"No," said Iain, "I can't see it at all. It's just a big mound of snow."

"I thought that," said Blinder in a satisfied voice. "I thought you wouldn't be able to see it."

Hand in hand they trudged on through the snow for what seemed to Iain to be ages, and then Blinder said, "The well is to your left. It's a few yards over there. But I'm sure it will be frozen over."

"Is that where it is?" said Iain.

"Yes," said Blinder, "it's over to your left. You keep over to this side with me."

"Right then," said Iain in his adult voice.

"We won't go near it," said Blinder, "in case anything happens." His blind empty eyes, unaffected by the sun, stared straight ahead of him.

After a while they were a good bit out of the village and Blinder stopped and said to Iain, "Now tell me what you can see."

"I can see the houses," said Iain, "and they are all covered with snow. Their roofs are covered with snow and even the doors have snow on them. I can see smoke rising from the chimneys. I can see birds on the telegraph wires. I can see the fences covered with snow. And that's all I can see."

"Is that all?" said Blinder with the same note of satisfaction in his voice. "Is that all you can see?"

"Yes," said Iain.

"Well then," said Blinder," I think we should go back," and he started to hum under his breath as if he was happy. All the way back to his house he was humming while the two of them hand in hand swam through the snow which was practically up to their knees, and now and again Iain heard the cock crow and then a dog bark till another dog answered the first dog and then there was a whole lot of invisible dogs barking all over the village.

6

ONE EVENING IAIN went to see the Cook in order to ask him what the weather was going to be like the following day as he, his mother and Kenneth, were going to town, which they did only once a year because they had not much money. Nobody knew why he was called the Cook, though perhaps he might have been one in his youth when he was sailing the oceans on a merchant ship. He was an old man now, with a white beard and red cheeks, and he smoked a small stubby pipe.

He was sitting on a bench outside his house when Iain called on him, and taking his pipe out of his mouth, he said, "Hullo, Iain, where have you been for such a long time? I haven't seen you for weeks."

"I wasn't doing anything," said Iain. "Nothing particular."

The Cook's teeth were yellow because of the tobacco he smoked and there was a smell from his clothes which Iain could never identify.

"I came to ask you," said Iain, and then he stopped, for the Cook had begun to speak.

"You never come without asking for something," he said. "Why don't you come and see me anyway?"

As Iain didn't have an answer to this he didn't say anything: but the answer that he might have given if he had been bold enough was that he didn't very much like talking to old people, for he didn't know what to say and a lot of the time he used to sit on a chair looking down at his feet and kicking them together while he could hear the clock ticking, and he couldn't think of any excuse for leaving. Anyway old people asked silly questions, and sometimes they would sit for hours without saying anything at all.

He began again. "I came to ask you if it is going to be a good day tomorrow." The words came out with a rush and then he stopped abruptly.

"Aye aye," said the Cook. " I know what you're going to do. You're going to town. All the boys who are going to town ask me about the weather. I know that. Well, then," he said, pointing at the sky with his pipe, "do you see that? It's got straight clouds in it." Iain looked at the sky and sure enough it was barred with clouds above the hill that would later turn purple, as it always did, in the evening.

"Is that a good sign then?" he said, wishing that the Cook would give him a definite answer so that he could get away.

"Well, in a way yes, and in another way no," said the Cook. "Aren't you the lucky one to be going to town? When I was your age I never got to town at all. And anyway in those days they didn't have buses, they just had gigs and horses." As it hadn't occurred to Iain that the Cook could ever have been young he waited politely for him to finish speaking, only wondering why old people couldn't answer yes or no to a simple question.

"That's right," said the Cook, tapping the pipe on his knee, "we used to have gigs. And do you know how I spent my time when I was young? I used to help my father with the ploughing. And I used to fish. You're still in school, aren't you? Well I left school when I was twelve and I never went back. The only time I asked about the weather was when I used to fish. Ay, those were the days. And we used to have ceilidhs too. We used to go to people's houses and sing songs till late at night. That's how we spent the time." And he paused as if he was seeing what he was talking about, and seemed to have forgotten the pipe which was now lying motionless in his wrinkled hand.

"I used to be like you once," said the Cook. "Did you know that? I was your age once. You wouldn't think that now, would you, but I was exactly your age. In those days the sky was clearer and we never hardly had any storms or rain. We used to run barefoot on the moors and the hills and I once found a bird's nest: it was a skylark's nest and it had three speckled eggs in it, and they were warm. We were doing the peats at the time and I was coming home with my wheelbarrow full of peats when I saw the nest. I had very keen eyesight when I was young: I'm still not bad yet. People will tell you that we didn't have any enjoyments but they're wrong. The air was fresher in those days, Iain, and the sea was bluer. What do you do with yourself anyway?"

Iain saw the Cook's wife come out of the house and empty a basin of water into the grass. She was old and small and wrinkled and she smiled at him and then she went back into the house again carrying her basin. The Cook hadn't turned to look at her at all: perhaps he hadn't seen her.

"I go to school," said Iain.

"School, eh? When I went to school the headmaster would belt us for the smallest thing. He belted me once because I didn't know my poetry. I can't remember now what the poetry was but he gave me six of the belt and he said, Perhaps that will teach you to remember. Eh eh? He was a small man with a red face and he was a very good headmaster. If I had gone home to my parents and told them that he had belted me they would have whipped me too, so I never said anything. He was a very respectable man, that headmaster, I can tell you that. But I didn't know then what I know now." He paused, and there was a long silence. Iain was going to ask him again about the weather but he didn't dare do so till the Cook himself would remember to tell him.

"Another thing," said the Cook, "we used to throw stones at each other. Did you do that? We used to line up, the boys from the two villages, and we used to throw stones. Big stones too. How they never killed anyone I don't know. We had teams, you know. But I don't suppose you do that now."

"No," said Iain.

"I thought not," said the Cook, "I thought not. I thought you wouldn't do that. Take that corn now. It used to be yellower than that. Even the corn isn't as yellow as it was. And the grass isn't as green. I remember the day when the grass was as green as . . ." And the Cook paused as if he couldn't find a comparison for the greenness of the grass. "And we used to run about barefoot and the grass would be warm under your feet. People don't run about barefoot now, they've all got shoes, but are they any better for that, eh?" And he glared fiercely at Iain as if he were about to strike him.

"Eh?" he added again, shaking his pipe vigorously to shake the ash out.

"The weather," said Iain at last, feebly.

"Eh?" said the Cook again, as if he were emerging out of a dream into which he had sunk. "Weather, eh? The weather was much better. Look at that sky. That sky isn't as bright as it used to be. Now, I'll tell you a funny thing about the weather. When you're as old as I am it's always cold but when you're young it's always warm. You remember that. Now take the sky, the sky is what you make it. Do you understand that? What is the sky? In the daytime you see the sun in the sky, isn't that right, and in the night time you see the moon. But who knows what the sky is like? Can your teachers tell you what the sky is? Tell me that. You tell me that. You ask them. They don't know either. Nobody knows what the sky is. Sometimes the sky is green and sometimes it's black. I'll tell you what the sky is. The sky is just a reflection, that's all it is. The sky above the sea is blue when the sea is blue and when the sea is grey the sky is grey. That's the sky for you. If you want to know about the sky you come to me. I know all about it. And I'll tell you

something else, the more I see of the sky the more I get puzzled. When you see it's green, that's because the earth is green. And there are caves in the sky too, and there are roads. The sky is a country of its own. You can turn a corner in the sky though you might not think it. I've made a study of the sky. Sometimes it seems to know what you are thinking. Have you ever noticed that? I don't suppose you have. That's because you're not sitting here like me. But it can. Sometimes when you're happy the sky is happy and sometimes when you're sad the sky is sad, and sometimes when you've nothing to do the sky has nothing to do. That's the sky for you."

As if he felt that he would never get away from the Cook if he didn't get an answer immediately, Iain rushed out the words, "What kind of day will it be tomorrow, sir?"

"Sir, eh," said the Cook. "That will be what they're teaching you at school, eh. Sir, eh?" But he seemed pleased just the same. Then with a keen look at Iain that penetrated right through him, he said, smilingly, "I'll tell you, Iain, it will be a good day tomorrow. It will be a very good day. It will be hot and there will be no clouds. Are you listening to me?"

"Yes," said Iain.

"Are you hearing me?" And his face came closer and closer so that Iain could see the red network of veins in his eyes. "It will be a good day tomorrow, boy. You remember that."

Iain stood up. "Thank you, sir," he said, and ran away as quickly as he could, only looking back once to see that the Cook was still sitting on his bench, the pipe back in his mouth, and staring straight ahead of him at the corn which was not so yellow as it once had been in the past.

Yet he was quite confident that the Cook would sort the sky out for him one way or another, for he was old enough to do that, and wise enough too.

7

IAIN AND KENNETH stood at the plank waiting for the bus to appear over the brae. It was nine in the morning and there was a blue haze over the ground though the grass was still wet. They were both dressed in brown woollen suits which their mother had knitted for them and there were tie pins at their throats. Their stomachs were uneasy with excitement which they relieved by kicking at the little stones of the road with their highly polished black shoes.

Suddenly Iain saw the big red lumbering bus appearing over the top of the brae and he ran up the path to the house shouting to his mother to come, for he was desperately frightened that the bus might leave without them. She appeared slowly, dressed in black and carrying her black handbag in her gloved right hand, while Kenneth was shouting from the foot of the path, "Hurry up hurry up," and dancing on the road with frustration. Their mother shut the door behind her, though she did not bother to lock it (for no one ever stole anything from the village houses), and then was walking down the path, Iain running ahead of her, as if escorting her, and now and then turning his head to see if she was still there. She had arrived at the plank when the bus stopped with a great creaking of brakes, the driver looking down from his seat, his foot still on the clutch. Their mother climbed into the bus first, followed by Kenneth and Iain, and then the bus set off, leaving the village behind it.

Iain sat in a seat by himself while in front of him his mother and Kenneth sat together. He was watching through the window everything that he could see, the scarred peat banks near the road, the houses which were still quiet and sleepy, the people waiting at the side of the road at the bus stops, the fields of corn which were golden under the sun now beginning to break through the haze. Now and again he would put his hand in his pocket to make sure that the money which had been given him was still there. He also had two shillings which had been given him by Mrs Macleod who stayed next door to them and for whom he often ran messages.

The bus lumbered on, the driver now and again leaning sideways from his seat to accept parcels from people who appeared at the side of the road, spoke to him a little and then disappeared as quickly as they had come. Iain thought that the driver was like a god looking down at them from his throne, dressed in his navy blue uniform. He always eased the clutch with such royal confidence, not looking down at all, but merely gazing ahead of him through the window. Iain wished more than anything to be like the driver but knew somehow that he would never have that confidence, that careless smiling poise. An old woman with parcels appeared beside him and he moved closer to the window, through which he could see Kenneth peering. Their mother, however, clutching her handbag, stared straight ahead of her without moving, only now and then telling Kenneth to be still.

Hurry up, hurry up, Iain was telling the bus in an undertone, almost as if it were a huge awkward animal that could understand what he was saying. But the bus kept to its stately pace, often stopping while more and more people climbed on, and through the window Iain could see men with scythes making their way down to the fields. Sometimes they would turn and wave and their scythes would flash in the sun which was now glittering on the window panes.

Finally, Iain knew that they were approaching the town, for there were more houses, there were fewer fields, and he could see tall dirty buildings belching smoke, and smell odd smells which he could not identify but which were very strong. They were like the rotten smells from old fish which were decaying in the middle of the smoke. They passed what looked like a school though the playground was empty as it was a Saturday; and then the bus had turned a corner past the cinema and it was moving slowly and steadily to its resting place on the pier. And there was the town in front of them, with seagulls flying above it, and the multitude of shops, and the sea with its fishing boats.

Soon the three of them were standing on the stone pier and Iain and Kenneth, their mother close behind them, went and looked at the fishing boats whose masts were like a forest of trees climbing out of the sea. They read the names of the boats rapturously, the *Sea Eagle*, the *Swallow*, the *Good Hope*, the *Water Baby* and saw these reflected swayingly in the water as in a continuously moving mirror. They saw too the slim masts and the ropes reflected, and on the decks they saw the orange buoys and the green nets. On the pier were boxes of fish and standing beside them, now and again pecking lazily and absent-mindedly at the bones of herring lying on the quay, were the seagulls, some of them with red spots on their beaks like drops of blood. Across the water they could see the castle standing among the woods with its white stony towers.

"Come on," said their mother, and they set off for the town.

There were so many people on the pavements that at first Iain and Kenneth stayed very close to their mother, but as time passed she would have to stop now and then in order to tell them to hurry up. They found themselves in shops where the smell of apples was almost overpowering as they nestled redly, in their boxes, among straw. They were each given an ice-cream cone whose coldness froze their teeth with the most delicious pain. They stood impatiently beside their mother as she stopped and talked at what seemed interminable length to friends of hers whom she had not seen for years, themselves in from the country for a day, and all of them wearing black coats and black hats. They peered in at the windows of the toy shops and once Iain found himself in a bookshop where he would have stayed for a long time reading *Answers* and *Titbits*, if his mother hadn't pulled him away to a clothes shop where they had to stand for hours among mirrors while she studied a black hat which at the end of it all she didn't even buy; and all the time as she turned the black hat over and over in her hand Iain could see through the shop door the people passing, the seagulls flying, and the castle towering and white in the distance across the river.

It was about midday when Kenneth saw the toy horse in the window. It was large, shiny and brown, with brown tassels for reins running along it. It stood lightly in the window as if it were ready to set off somewhere, completely on its own, riderless and free, its head raised proudly, even though the bit was in its mouth. The light of the sun shining directly on it made it appear fluid and animated, as if it were composed not of wood but of a powerful energetic substance akin to light itself; and its hooves hardly seemed to touch the wood on which it rested among the dolls, the teddy bears, the squirrels, all dominated by its playful hauteur.

"I want it," said Kenneth, standing at the window and dancing up and down. "I want it. I want the horse."

His mother tugged at his hand, looking round her in embarrassment and then leaning down to speak to him in a fierce whisper.

But Kenneth was pressing his nose against the window, his little body trembling with rage and greed, while some of the passers-by looked at him in amusement, and his mother felt more and more conspicuous.

"You can't have it," she told him in the same fierce whisper. "It's too expensive. We can't afford it."

But Kenneth kept on shouting, "I want it, I want it. It's mine," while his face grew redder and redder with rage. It was as if he could see himself already riding the horse to some secret destination of his own, while his mother was unfairly holding him back with her black gloved hands.

"You can't have it," she insisted, trying to drag him away, but he was so fierce and strong that she could hardly move him, and when her effort to pull him raised him slightly in the air he was kicking his heels as if he were a fish struggling at the end of a rod.

And at that moment Iain had a strange vision. He saw his mother dressed in black wrestling with his brother and he realised as if for the very first time that they were poor, that they were really poor, and as if with horror and embarrassment he saw his mother's worn black gloves, with a darn on the right one, and he wished that he could run away and hide. But also as he looked at his mother's agonised embarrassed face, its thinness and its pallor, he was moved by such intense pity that he turned to Kenneth and said angrily, "You shut up. You can't have it. Don't be such a fool." Kenneth looked at him open-mouthed as if the criticism of his behaviour were coming from a quarter that he couldn't at first identify, and then he burst into tears of rage and madness which were only relieved by a man stopping and giving him sixpence. Then the three of them walked on in silence, their mother now and again saying, "This is the last time I'll take you to town. I've a good mind to take you home on the one o'clock bus." But they didn't go home on the one o'clock bus though the threat seemed powerful enough to quieten Kenneth at least for that time.

In fact after they had had their lunch in an Italian café, the two of them went to the cinema, leaving their mother to wander round the shops. They paid their money at the desk and walked together into the blackness which was only illuminated by the usherette's torch. Finally they found themselves side by side among others of their own age gazing at the screen which was showing the title of the film as they entered, written as if on a certificate.

43

It was a Western and they watched in wonder as the cowboy rode over the hill into the town, hitched his horse to a post on the street, and entered the saloon where someone was thumping a piano, and girls in their flounced dresses were dancing or putting their arms around unshaven men. They saw the crooked sheriff in the pay of the saloon-keeper order the cowboy out of town and tell him that his brother had deserved everything he had got. They knew that the cowboy wouldn't leave, though he pretended to, and when he was ambushed by the saloon-keeper's employees among the rocks and cactus trees on his way to what had apparently been his brother's ranch, they knew that he wouldn't be killed. Imprisoned by the crooked marshal, he broke out, with the help of one of the saloon girls. Framed for a murder which he hadn't committed, it seemed that at last the forces ranged against him were too strong.

The ending was all that they could have wished, the cowboy alone against the crooked marshal, the saloon-keeper and two of his men, shooting it out in a barn and finally on the street itself. Then there came the final music on the swell of which the cowboy, tall in the saddle, rode out of town having avenged his brother's murder. Either of them would have done that for the other and they each thought how they might do it, strong and firm and righteous, guns strapped to their sides, rolling slightly from side to side on their high-heeled boots in Wyoming or Texas.

They were curiously silent as they walked out of the cinema into the dazzling daylight, passing people on the pavement as if they were still in the Western town, and prepared to see horses being tied to posts and wagons rocking down the street.

As they walked along to meet their mother, the world was sparkling with images from the film they had just seen. Kenneth had forgotten all about his toy horse and was engaged with larger horses of his imagination. Then from a distance they saw their mother in her black coat waiting patiently on a bench by the sea, her few purchases by her side. Strolling towards her in the Western sun which shone red beyond her above the sea, Iain again experienced the same feeling of sorrow, for his mother looked so subdued and solitary sitting there, not as yet seeing them but gazing out at the water as if she had always been there and would always remain there in the same position. She looked so frail and black and lonely amongst all the passing traffic of the town that he suddenly said in a rough voice to Kenneth, "Come on, she's expecting us," and the two of them raced towards their mother who suddenly looked up and saw them and rose from her seat as if transformed.

"You've been a long time," she said reproachfully.

"The picture only finished just now," said Kenneth angrily as if ready to start a quarrel again.

Iain didn't say anything. But when later as they were going home on the bus she told him to straighten his tie, he felt bad-tempered as if he didn't think she had any right to be giving him orders.

He sat in silence during most of the journey home, thinking of the film and especially of the part where the cowboy had left the town for the last time, and the music had grown louder and louder. In his mind's eye he watched the horse and rider disappearing over the hill into the distance and wished he could do the same.

"I bought you two chocolate mice," said his mother later as she was unwrapping her few parcels.

"You and Kenneth have them," said Iain, "you have them." And though he would dearly have liked one of the chocolate mice himself he was happy to watch them eating them, happier than he had been in town. But still, another whole year, and he would go again.

8

ONE DAY IAIN and Daial went into an empty thatched house that was in the village, the rusty-hinged wooden door creaking as they entered. They stood silently in the main room in which there was an old bench that had fallen over and smelt the tang of musty straw which prickled their nostrils.

"Hey," said Daial, "look up there." When Iain looked up he was gazing straight at the sky, for much of the roof had gone and all they could see were ancient planks and rafters that seemed half burnt.

In the sky he could see the white clouds moving. The old house with its smell of smoke and straw felt weird as if part of it remained alive though it appeared dead and desolate, and once Daial had a great fright for when he thrust his head through a paneless window he found himself staring straight at a cow which was placidly gazing into the room, while chewing grass in its brown jaws.

"Whoosh," he shouted in a high voice. "Whoosh," and the cow withdrew its head and ambled away, its tail swinging lazily.

They found a jam jar, an old blue plate, and a box in which there was a variety of nuts and bolts in which Iain wasn't interested, though Daial was, for he had got himself a new bicycle which he had left leaning against the stone wall of the house. After a while Iain got bored and left him kneeling in the room, his small black head bent over the box, rummaging among the nuts, while he himself pushed aside the torn drape that separated the two rooms of the house and entered the bedroom.

In this room there was an old bed with clothes on it that had once been white but which were now damp and mouldy, shining faintly in the twilight created by the torn curtains.

Iain stood uncertainly in the middle of the room and gazed at the faint white pillows and faint white sheets in a silence that lapped like water round the cracked mirror and the one chair and the ancient dressing table which was sunk into a hollow of the floor. It was as if he had found himself in an underwater cave far from the traffic of the world, noiseless and eerie. As he turned and looked in the mirror which was on a wall facing the bed, a strange thing happened. In the cracked glass he saw a face which was not his own, and this face, broken and grained, was the face of an old woman with no teeth. Iain swung round, unable to speak or scream, and there, sitting upright in the bed, in a veil of cobwebs, her grained hands on the sheet in front of her, was a very old woman, so old that her face seemed hardly human. She wasn't looking at Iain at all, but down at the bed as if she was holding in her hands a plate which was invisible to the frightened gazing boy.

And then out of the silence she began to speak, her mouth making hissing sounds because she had no teeth, her bald head thrust out of her ragged nightgown.

"My food," she was saying, "my food. Where is my food? No one brings me any food. You want me to die. That's why you don't bring me any food. I want my food. I used to bring you your food but you don't bring me any. Do you remember when you were young I would bring you your food. Why don't you?" And it seemed that tears coursed down her face, as she wove her hands together. "I wouldn't do this to you. When you were young I brought you your food but you want me to die. Well, it won't be long now. And you'll suffer for it. I hope you suffer and rot in hell." And her hands came together as if she were squeezing something to death, a network of blue veins standing out on them, hard and coarse.

"I hate you," she said in the same hissing voice. "I hate all of

47

you. I told you not to marry him. I told you he was a drunkard and a waster. But no, you wouldn't listen, would you. You knew best, didn't you? And now he won't give me any food, he says he has no money. You should make him. But he's stronger than you. He's stronger than us." And her voice changed and became pleading like that of a child, monotonous and peevish. "Please give me my food, my tea. He won't know. Don't be frightened of him. God will look after you. You're my daughter, aren't you. What are you doing? I gave you your food when you were young, when you were a baby. I did." And her eyes became small and cunning. "I did. I fed you. You had the best food there was. You shouldn't have married him. I hate him. Stay with me. Why don't you stay with me?" And she rose slowly in the bed and stretched out her hands towards the invisible daughter and her mouth was a wide hole without teeth and her hands were veined with hard blue veins that stood out from the flesh, and her throat was as scraggy as that of an old hen.

In the twilight of the room Iain backed away against the dressing table, against the mirror, so that the dressing table toppled over and he fell down on top of it.

And then the woman's hands were on him as if she wished to strangle him, and in her eyes there was a crazy triumphant light, and it was as if she was emerging out of an old rotten net of cobwebs, and at that moment Iain screamed and screamed, and there was Daial standing at the torn drape looking down at Iain lying on the floor.

"What happened?" he said to Iain. "What happened? Did you fall?" Iain staggered out of the mad dream, seeing above him Daial's white healthy teeth and above them the sky with the white clouds racing past over the scorched rafters and the scanty straw.

"I'm all right," he said. "I'm all right. I just fell." The bed was again uninhabited, the pillows unwrinkled, the mirror without reflection.

48

As if he had forgotten all about the scream, Daial said, "Look what I found. It's a nut for a bicycle," and held it out in his hand as if he were offering it as a gift to Iain. "See it? I can use that."

"Very good," said Iain, "very good."

He made his way over the toppled dressing table and past the cracked mirror to the other room and then out into the fresh air, breathing it deeply into his lungs, and glancing briefly at the window of the bedroom lest he should see an old face at it. When he turned away again the village lay before him, quiet and normal, smoke rising from the chimneys of the houses, men and women working in the fields.

"Come on, then," he said to Daial. The two of them walked to the main road, Daial pushing his bicycle along beside him. When they reached the road Iain said, "Can you give me a spin on your bike?"

When Daial said that he could Iain raced away at full speed, feeling the wind blowing his hair about, pedalling furiously as if he were escaping from something which had a smell of burnt straw, smoking timbers, and a deeper smell even than that, the smell of old rotten clothes and old rotten flesh, the smell of the grave itself.

9

IT WAS A Saturday morning and Iain was in the house of Andy Macleod, known as Speedy and one of the best footballers in the village. There was going to be a big football match that afternoon between Iain's own village and the neighbouring village, a match that was considered to be the most important event in the year. Speedy who played centre forward was in the house by himself as his father and mother and sisters were out stacking the corn, and indeed Iain could see them through the window, bending down and gathering the sheaves in their arms. Their movements were curiously stylised and distant, as if they belonged to people he didn't know, or as if they could have belonged to anyone. Speedy was trying on his white shorts, bright green shirt, his green stockings and his yellow football boots. He was very stocky and his legs were hairy. Now and again with a careless gesture he would toss his hair back from his strong bulletlike head.

"Do you think we'll win?" said Iain.

"Of course we'll win," said Speedy who was tying his laces. "No problem." He stood up and kicked out with his football boots at an imaginary ball, but the floor was so polished that he nearly fell over, only regaining his balance just in time.

"Bugger you," he said. And then after a while, "Mind you, it's very hard."

"What's very hard?" said Iain curiously, happy and astonished that Speedy wished to speak to him at all.

"It's hard to keep your form," said Speedy. "You see, Iain, it's like this. If you're good they expect you to be good all the time.

You score two goals one week and then they expect you to score two goals next week as well." He went over to a mirror and stood in front of it, passing his hand across his hair, and snapping the elastic of his shorts.

"That's the thing you must remember. Now take me. Last year I scored three goals and they'll expect me to do the same this year. It's a great responsibility."

"I can see that," said Iain gravely.

"Now take it if you're nervous," said Speedy, turning away from the mirror. "You can't get the ball to do what you want it to do. And if you don't get a good kick at the beginning of the game then you're no good for the rest of it. That's another thing they don't understand. Now last year I knew everything was going to be all right from the beginning of the game, but this year . . ."

He went over to the window, as if to make sure that none of his family was coming back into the house, and then opened a cupboard from which he took a half bottle of whisky, and poured out a glass for himself. He sat down in a chair drinking it.

"You see, Iain, I haven't played for a year. I was working at the fishing and I never got a chance to practise and you know what they're like here. If we lose it's the end of the world. It's a great responsibility." And he drank a little more whisky.

"Do you think you'd get a trial for a club?" said Iain who supported Rangers.

"I might, I might at that. It's all a matter of whether you're spotted or not. That's where the thing is. If there's a scout watching you you might get a trial. There are as good players playing with me as you would get in a club."

"Do you get nervous then?"

"No. I don't get nervous much. Some of them get nervous. If you get nervous you're no good. You miss the ball or your passes go all wrong. Say just now I had the ball here," said Speedy, getting to his feet, "and I wanted to pass it over to where you are.

Well, the ball might go to the other chair there. That's if you're nervous. Do you see that?"

"Yes," said Iain. "I see that."

"And then you see," said Speedy, sitting down again, "your stomach would be all upset. That wouldn't be good for you either." And he drank some more whisky. "If I go out there today and I'm nervous I won't be any good and they'll say 'Speedy's over the hill. He can't do it any longer.' Well, I don't want them to say that because you have your pride. And your confidence. If your confidence goes you're finished." He stood up suddenly and walked about the room, looking at some photographs that were on the sideboard, and then sat down again.

"And your girl friend might be there." He became silent for a while, staring into the fireplace. "If your girl friend is there and you make a fool of yourself you don't like it. And then on Monday morning when you go to your work your mates will start making jokes. But it's not them who have the responsibility. It's easy for them to speak. It's no joke."

Iain didn't know what girl friends had to do with football but accepted that if Speedy mentioned them then he must have some reason for doing so.

"But there won't be any problem. We'll beat them right enough," said Speedy and drank some more whisky, gazing afterwards into the glass as if he were seeing some disagreeable picture there. Then he began to cross and uncross his legs and to take deep breaths which he slowly expelled.

It occurred to Iain that football was a much more complicated game than he had thought if you had to consider all the things that Speedy was talking about.

"It's like this," said Speedy wrinkling his brow as if he were concentrating. "You're the centre forward and everything depends on you. You're the one who has to get the goals. Say the goal is in front of you and you miss, then people will start shouting, and making a fool of you. The forward line is much worse off than the defence. The defence don't have to get goals."

And he got to his feet and stood in the middle of the floor as if he were making a speech, while Iain noticed that his face had become redder. "Everything depends on you, you understand. The whole village depends on you." He poured out some more whisky and then went, rolling slightly on his football boots, into the scullery and swished some water into the glass. After he had come back he looked keenly at Iain and said: "If I was you I wouldn't go to the match."

"Not go to the match?" Iain echoed.

"That's right," said Speedy decisively. "It won't be any good this year. Too many of the players haven't been practising. Take me now. I haven't had any practice. If I was you I would stay away. That's what I would do."

"But . . ." Iain began.

"I'm telling you," said Speedy earnestly, "it won't be as good as last year. It's all a question of practice, you see. If I had my way nobody would go to the match except the players, and then you would get a good game. That's my opinion anyway." He stopped at the window and stared out moodily at his father and mother and sisters who were still monotonously and relentlessly gathering sheaves in their arms and building the stack. It was as if standing there in his white and green he envied them the slow certain job that they were doing, its gradual inevitability.

"I'm going anyway," said Iain, "and all the other boys are going."

"And they're all expecting me to score goals," said Speedy angrily. "I know that. They all want to be like Speedy, eh? Isn't that right? But they don't know the responsibility. They think that all you have to do is go out on the pitch and score goals. Isn't that right, eh?"

"I don't know," said Iain who was beginning to feel puzzled and rather frightened.

"But I know," said Speedy. "I was the same. There was a footballer when I was your age and he was nicknamed Delaney and he used to score goals all the time. And then one day he lost his form just like that," and he snapped his fingers quickly. "And they booed him. They booed him because he couldn't score any more goals. And yet he had scored a lot of goals before that. But they forgot about that, do you see? And he was still the same fellow, do you understand?" His brow wrinkled as if he were concentrating deeply. "He was still the same fellow and he had scored all those goals but now because he couldn't score any more they booed him. He was a tall fellow with very long legs. He wasn't like me at all, he was very different from me in his style of play." He fell silent again staring into his glass. "He was drowned on a fishing boat. Nobody knows what happened but they found his body washed ashore. Anyway what I was going to say, they shout at you and tell you, 'If you were only as good as Delaney.' They remember him now, you see, but when he was alive they forgot about him." And he kicked out viciously as if at an imaginary ball. "That's people for you."

He took another long breath, expelled it slowly, and then stretched out his hand in front of him, studied it, and put it down again on his knee.

"Now I'm telling you, don't go. It won't be any good. And you tell your friends not to go either. After all it's only a game, isn't it. It's not the end of the world. Someone's got to win and someone's got to lose."

"I suppose so," said Iain doubtfully and when he looked out of the window he saw Stork, who had a wooden leg, limping along the road on his way to the game. He had to leave home earlier than other people because of his wooden leg, and as he hobbled along Iain could see his outthrust jaw, his pale face and his angry staring eyes. The thing was, Stork would never take a lift, or accept help from anybody, and he lived on his own in a perpetual resentful silence. But when he arrived on the touchline of a football pitch he became completely transformed, and would shout insults, admonitions, frenzied encouragement at the players, and sometimes he would scream obscenities at the referee for giving perfectly fair decisions against his team. For this he was greatly respected, and as he had a wooden leg he was perfectly safe from any consequences that might have followed from his behaviour. After the match was over he would relapse into his angry resentful silence, and finally hobble away, wincing, towards his empty house.

"There's Stork," said Iain, without thinking.

"That old fool. He should stay at home," said Speedy. "He thinks he's an expert but he doesn't know anything. He's just making a fool of himself, that's all he's doing."

He went over to the cupboard and poured himself another whisky and then said in a more good-humoured voice, as he sat down on his chair in front of the mirror, "It depends on the start you get. That's what it depends on."

Iain got to his feet and said, "I'm going home to my dinner now." He didn't like to see Speedy sitting there drinking whisky and wearing his football kit at the same time. In fact he wished that he hadn't come. He would far rather have seen Speedy emerging out of the crowd, running on to the field in his green and white, and taking his first shot at goal.

As he stood at the door he could see Stork plodding steadily and irresistibly into the distance, and in his mind's eye he simultaneously pictured Speedy on the football pitch, swerving to the right and hitting the ball so viciously that it soared high into the air, entering the net in the top right-hand corner.

He kept the image in his mind as he walked home because it seemed to him to be the best one that he could think of, and much more real than the Speedy he had just seen, more real even than Speedy's parents and sisters bending down as they gathered the sheaves of corn and stacked them. But what really bothered him was that Speedy had talked to him so much: adults didn't usually speak to him at such length. He would have felt much happier if Speedy hadn't spoken to him at all, if he hadn't explained so much to him, if he had just given him orders or told him to go home, that he was too busy. That would really have been much more like the Speedy that he thought he knew.

10

IN THE NEXT village there lived Iain's uncle who had a croft, from which they got some potatoes, as a tiny part of the potato field was set aside for Iain's mother. He had a larger house than Iain's mother had, and a barn in which there were old pieces of harness made of leather hanging on the whitewashed walls, hay lofts, and a byre in which the cows were dark presences among brown rivulets and channels.

Iain didn't like his uncle much, for he had a red face and staring eyes and unshaven cheeks which he sometimes rubbed against Iain's smoother ones. He preferred his aunt who had very white hair, and always smelt of flour. His uncle used to sit in his chair and say, "I don't know what these schools are coming to. When I was your age, Iain, I was doing a man's work on the croft." And he would look angrily at his sister, Iain's mother, who didn't say anything as she needed the potatoes.

One day after they had been picking potatoes and had come home, tired and sore, his uncle whose name was Angus took him into the barn where the haylofts were. "There are mice in there," he said to Iain. "I know they're there and I can't stand them." In the half-light of the barn his red face looked fierce and clear, almost like a cockerel's, and his bald head shone like a stone that has been polished by the action of water for many years.

Iain sometimes thought that in the same way as he didn't like his uncle so his uncle didn't like him and wished somehow to humiliate him, as that every day he had been making comments, like, "Iain's just a scholar. He doesn't know how to use the spade.

You're not teaching the boy right, Agnes. You should make a man of him. What's he going to be, eh? Tell me that." And his mother said nothing, ignoring her brother as best she could for the sake of the potatoes.

All this time Iain felt his courage draining away from him as his foot rested on the spade and in the distance he could see his uncle's black bull pacing restlessly on his tether, and now and then coming to a halt like a statue of solid black stone.

His uncle stood in the half-light of the barn staring into the hay, the blue straps of his dungarees over his blue shirt. "Pss, pss, pss," he suddenly said and there appeared as if by magic at his side a large golden cat which arched its back lazily and gazed up at him with a languid loving gaze.

"Get 'em," said Iain's uncle and he threw the cat in among the hay. Suddenly before Iain's astonished and horrified eyes there was an explosion of activity, the hay stirred and seethed like porridge bubbling in a pot, and there was the cat emerging out of it carrying a large fat grey mouse in its mouth.

"Watch this now," said his uncle. "You watch this." And as Iain watched, the cat came over to his uncle with the mouse and dropped it beside his rough leather boots. It lay crouched on the floor watching the mouse intently, now and again pushing out a paw and touching it, its eyes gleaming in the half-darkness, while at the same time Iain sensed that his uncle was staring at him with his angry face.

Once while the cat was staring sleepily into space, its eyes blinking serenely, the mouse, as if sensing an opportunity for escape, made a sudden scamper, but the cat as quick as lightning put out its paw and drew it towards it and then remained intent as before without moving. The four of them – his uncle, Iain, the cat and the mouse – remained like this for a long time, as if they were carved on a frieze, in a motionlessness that was not inactivity but rather activity throbbing with tension, inactivity carried to an

extreme of activity, as if the barn were a battlefield on which two armies, immersed in fighting, had paused, locked in each other's arms, in an intensity of the kind that is possible only to the fiercest of combatants.

As Iain watched, the mouse made another attempt to escape and again the cat, golden-bodied, golden-eyed, put out its paw playfully and pulled it back. Then it turned the mouse over as if it were inspecting it, as if it were some strange being that it hadn't seen before, and finally flicked it up in the air.

Iain's uncle said in a flat voice, "It has broken its back." Then he and Iain left the barn.

When they were outside Iain suddenly began to beat his uncle with his fists and shout, "I hate you, I hate you, I hate you." His voice rose in a scream so high that the bull turned its black massive stony head and looked at them, before slowly bending it to the earth again. "I hate you, I hate you, I hate you," Iain was shouting, beating his fists against his uncle's body.

"What's wrong with you?" said his uncle in genuine surprise. "What's wrong with you?"

But Iain turned away from him and ran into the house and stood in front of his mother throbbing with rage and anguish, his face intensely pale. "I want to go home," he shouted to his mother. "I want to go home."

His aunt who had been sitting talking to his mother stood up and came over to him, stroking his hair and gazing at his uncle who was standing in the doorway and saying: "All that happened was that the cat killed a mouse."

"It wasn't, it wasn't," Iain screamed. "It wasn't that. You were . . ." His body throbbed with inarticulate rage, for he knew that more than that had happened, but he couldn't express what it was.

"I hate you," he screamed, stamping his foot on the floor. "Come home," he pleaded with his mother.

"Would he like a cup of tea," said his aunt to his mother.

"No, no, no," Iain screamed. "I want to go home."

His mother looked from Iain to her brother and she knew that at that moment she would have to make a choice which would be hard for her, the potatoes that she needed or her son. Her brother was looking at her with clear lazy eyes as if he recognised this, and also as if he knew in which direction she would jump, which road she would take: and as if he also knew that whatever direction she took he would be able to drag her back again into his richer circle. She looked around her at the house which was so much better than her own, at the easy chairs, the carpets, the ornaments on the mantelpiece, the cream-coloured clock, the house of a childless couple who had put all their earnings into the furniture.

Her sister-in-law hung limply between the two of them and her whiteness seemed to have turned to a diminished grey, as if she had suddenly become tiny and hump-backed, and a glaze had come over her eyes.

"I never liked you," said Agnes to her brother. "I never liked you. Ever. Even when we were young I never liked you. Our father never liked you either. I remember the time you broke my doll. No," she said to her sister-in-law, "I never wanted to say it, not about my own brother, but it's true. You think I want your potatoes. Well, I need them but I can do without them. You're always holding that over me, aren't you? When my husband died what did you do for me? Nothing. You never even came to visit me. And yet he was a better man than you. He was a sailor and he had seen the world. You haven't seen anything. Nothing but this croft and this house. For years I've been over in that village and you never came to visit me, and you're on at Iain because he's clever, because you're not clever yourself. I know you went to Australia and you threw in your job there because you couldn't do it and you came home here, and you took over the croft. I never liked you and I don't like you now."

"He's just a crybaby," said her brother, "that's all he is. You

61

can't bring him up, that's what's wrong with you. You let him do what he wants. Women can't bring up boys. Everyone knows that. It's books with him all the time. What use are books to him? Eh? Tell me that. If I had him I'd . . ."

"You keep your mouth shut, Angus," said his wife suddenly. "You just keep your mouth shut." And though she spoke strongly she was trembling. "You keep your mouth shut. You don't have an ounce of pity on your bones. She's right in what she's saying. You never had any children of your own and that's why you are what you are." She subsided into silence again and there they stood, the four of them, Iain and his uncle and his mother and his aunt, in the living room of that house which was much better than that of Iain's mother, and they were frozen momently in time as if the clock had stopped, and poison was running like rivulets from their mouths, while outside the window Iain could see the black bull raising its head, with spittle at its mouth and nostrils, solid in the day.

His mother got to her feet. "Come on, Iain," she said.

"Are you going then?" said her brother, as if he were surprised that she was escaping.

"I'm going and I'm not coming back," said Iain's mother. And she took Iain by the hand and led him past her brother who was standing in the doorway.

"All right then," he shouted, the veins standing out on his forehead. "But I'm telling you he's a crybaby. And it's high time you made a man of him."

"A man like you?" she said, raising her head scornfully.

"Yes," he shouted, "a man like me. I've got my own croft. I'm not a beggar."

As she was going out the door she raised her hand as if to slap him but then thought better of it and dropped it. Without a word she walked down the path to the gate, somehow succeeding in looking larger than her brother in her draggled clothes.

"Well, now we know where we are," she said to Iain. As she reached the gate she turned and shouted, "And you can keep your potatoes." Then the two of them walked away together, her hand still clutching Iain's hand. When Iain looked at her he saw her proud white face staring straight ahead of her, her back straight as a ruler, her lips clamped tightly together, and her boots, slightly cracked and clayey from the potato field, heavy on the road.

11

"WHAT WAS MY father like?" said Iain one day to his mother as she sat in her chair knitting while Iain sat on the floor with a picture book open in front of him.

"Your father? He was just like anyone else. He was a sailor."

"Where did he sail to?"

"He sailed all over the world."

"I know, but what places?"

"I can't remember all the places. I think he was in Australia and New Zealand. But I don't remember all the places."

"Was he always a sailor?"

"No, he wasn't always a sailor. We lived in Glasgow for a while. He used to be in the gasworks."

"The gasworks? What's that?"

"Just gasworks. Why do you want to know anyway?"

"Nothing. It just came into my head. Everyone else talks about their fathers. Petey's father was in the Navy."

Her fingers stopped their knitting and she said, "It's a long time since your father died. We were living in Glasgow at the time. He caught pneumonia and then he got TB and when they tried to keep the windows open he was always getting up and shutting them. I used to go and visit him. I would get the bus from Sauchiehall Street and I would take it to the hospital. He would sit up in bed and say to me, 'Another week or two, eh, and I'll be as good as new. I'll be out of here. I think I'll leave the gasworks and go back to the boats. The fresh air will do me good but I'm not having them keep the windows open all the time. All you get is a draught. You don't get the proper benefit of the air.' That's what he used to say, your father."

"Was he an officer?"

"He was a bosun and that's almost as good as an officer. He would bring things home, little presents, and I knew that . . ." She clamped her lips together as if she had decided not to say whatever she had been going to. "Anyway that was how he died."

After a while she said, "He was a good dancer. That was how we met, at a dance. He came up to me and he said, 'Would you care for this one?' And I danced with him. He was very light on his feet. When we lived in Glasgow we were in a tenement and we had good neighbours." She stared dully out at the day which was turning cloudy and said, "I liked Glasgow. A lot of people don't like Glasgow, they say it's too big and dirty, but I liked it. We had very good neighbours. The people there are very warm-hearted. If anything happened to you the others helped you. I used to go to the shops on Sauchiehall Street. We didn't have much money but I used to go and admire the shops. When your father had any money he would spend it right away. I used to tell him, 'Keep some of your money for your old age,' but he didn't keep any of it."

"Did he have a lot of money then?"

"No, he didn't. But what he had he spent. That was the way he was. I hope you're not going to be like that. When you grow up and earn money you should put it in a bank, and that way you'll never want."

"I want to be a sailor too," said Iain who was looking at his picture book in which he could see a big schooner becalmed on a blue sea. "I want to go away and see the world."

His mother looked at him for a moment in silence and then said, "Is that what you want to do?"

"But I would take you with me," said Iain earnestly.

"What good would I be on a ship?" said his mother, laughing so that her face was transformed as if the sun had come out from behind a cloud. "What would I do on a ship?"

"I would take you on a tour," said Iain. "I would take you on a tour round the world."

"One day he went out," she said, "and he didn't come back till night, and he'd brought some of his friends with him. He had met them in a pub, they were sailors, and they came from the island. He was very thoughtless that way because of his kind nature. And we didn't have any food in the house. They stayed all night and one of them had to sleep on the floor in the same room as your father, because we didn't have another room. I had no food at all and I was ashamed. But they didn't need any food, all they did was drink and sing. They went away in the morning, the first time anyone left a house of mine without eating. You see, in my father's time, when people came to the communions there was plenty of food. But we didn't have any food that night. I remember it well because I was so ashamed and your father said to me, 'Why didn't you give them something to eat?' He didn't know that there wasn't any food in the house. He never thought about things like that. That was why he was so popular. Come day, go day."

She had forgotten about Iain while she was talking and sat staring into the past as if she were gazing at a series of pictures in a book or on a moving screen and the pictures were so vivid that her eyes followed them intently as they passed in front of her eyes.

"I wonder if he was in Hong Kong," said Iain suddenly.

"Hong Kong?"

"Yes, it's in China and there's a picture of it here. It's got a lot of shops and there are Chinamen there."

"I don't know about that," said his mother. "I don't know about Hong Kong. Maybe he was. He was in a lot of places. He told me about a place where they left food for their dead people.

That might have been Hong Kong. He was very alive, you see, your father. I wondered . . ."

And again she clamped her lips together as if she had decided against saying something that she had intended to say. "It's not a good thing when a man is away so long. But he said that that was where the money was. He didn't like the gasworks. Sometimes on Saturdays we would go out into the country and we would visit Loch Lomond. He was quite happy there watching the boats sail up and down the loch. When he would come home at night he would start singing *Loch Lomond*, you know, the song." And her lips suddenly softened as if she were hearing her husband's voice as he stood in the kitchen in their tenement singing,

> "Where me and my true love will never meet again
> On the bonnie bonnie banks of Loch Lomond."

But of course she would never sing herself, she had never sung a song in her life and she wasn't going to start now, at her age.

Iain turned another page of his picture book and said, "Maybe he was in New York too."

"He might have been," said his mother, who after her moment of becalmment had gone back to her knitting. "Everyone liked your father. Only . . . But it doesn't matter. And you tell your friends that he was a bosun. He was always a good seaman."

Iain sat happily on the floor thinking about his father. His image of him was that of a sailor shouting orders to his men while they rushed about all over the decks or hauled at sails as the breeze propelled the ship through the hissing water on its way to the East. "Come on then, lads," his father would shout to them, "get a move on there." Kindly but firm, but able to deal with any of them if they became cheeky. "You know, my lad, that you have to take your orders like anyone else. Five lashes for him. We must have discipline on board this ship." Sometimes in a strange way his father's face faded into that of his mother and then became itself again.

"He loved children," said his mother. "He would tell them stories and when you were a baby he would take you on his shoulders and show you off to people. He would say, 'This boy is going to be far better than me. He won't waste his life as I did.' And then he would laugh and . . ." She fell silent again and then began to speak in quite a different voice. "But it's true just the same. He didn't think about anything really, not about food or rent or furniture or anything like that. He left all that to me. He left you to me as well. What he said about you was true in a way."

"What did he say, Mother?"

"Oh, nothing. He didn't say anything. He liked children, that was what I was saying."

I am Jim Hawkins and my father is captain of the good ship, the *Hispaniola*, and we are in search of treasure. My father can handle Long John Silver all right. To the hold with him and keep him there till he learns some sense. He's got to be disciplined. Don't give him food or water for three days. And then his father would shout, "Keep her going boys. Keep her on course. Steady as you go, you lubbers."

"He died a brave death, they said," his mother remarked, broodingly bent over her knitting. "The nurses told me that. His last words were, 'Shut that window, will you?' So they said. And the people in the tenement took a collection and gave me the money. That was a long time ago. They came into the house, six of them, and they pressed the money into my hand. They didn't wait for tea or anything. That must be, oh nine years ago. You were two at the time and Kenneth was one. Oh well, this won't do."

And she put the knitting away, got to her feet, and put the kettle on. "You'd better run to the shop and get some sugar." She counted out the pennies to him, and he ran down to the plank and then at full speed along the road towards the shop. She stood at the window watching him and thinking, I hope he won't turn out like his father. But while she was thinking that she was also thinking, I loved him and I miss him. She stared at Iain's diminishing figure till eventually like a small boat he disappeared over the horizon of the brae.

12

EVERY MORNING IAIN used to go to buy the milk from a woman called Big Dollag who lived with her two sons in a house which stood slightly back from the road at the bottom of the brae. Big Dollag was large and extremely deaf, and for this reason she shouted when she was talking to someone as if she was speaking through a high gale, her hand held to her right ear.

She would say to Iain, "Have you heard anything new, eh?" and he would shout back that he hadn't, and she would look at him in a disappointed manner, encased in her prison of almost total deafness.

One of her sons always sat in a corner of the kitchen, never speaking but smiling benevolently and hidden behind a green net which he seemed to be endlessly repairing, so that Iain thought of him as a pleasant spider who was weaving the net out of himself in some strange way.

Iain would stand in the scullery while Big Dollag poured the milk into his jug from a big red ewer and all the time she would be saying things like: "Who was that man who passed along the road yesterday? He was wearing a hat and he had an umbrella. Do you know who it was? I nearly went to speak to him but he went by too quickly."

And Iain would stand on the stone floor impatient to be gone, for he found it very exhausting and hard on his voice to converse with Big Dollag. She got the milk from a brown cow which she allowed to wander among the houses, sometimes chewing the washing that had been hung on ropes to dry. Once she had almost eaten Iain's own green jersey but his mother had said nothing to Big Dollag in case she stopped selling them the milk, for no one else would do so.

Iain found the house very strange because apart from the son who was always repairing the green net, another son would sometimes emerge from his room and then go back to it like a shy deer when he saw Iain. It seemed odd that the two sons should be so silent when Big Dollag herself was so noisy, her deep voice echoing through the house, and almost reverberating from the cold stone.

One morning when he had arrived for the milk as usual he found a stranger sitting in the kitchen by the fire which was, unusually, glowing brightly; and this stranger was wearing a coat, which Iain thought odd as he had never in his life seen someone doing so in a house before.

"That man you are seeing there," Big Dollag shouted, "is my son Jim. He is home from America. He came yesterday and he is not going back again."

Iain looked at the man shyly and the man in turn looked at him, and Iain saw that he had soft haunted eyes as if he had suffered a great deal.

"How are you, lad," said the man to him. "Who is he, Mother?" At first Dollag couldn't hear what he was saying, for his voice was even softer than Iain's, and it was only after some protracted verbal confusion that she eventually replied:

"He is Agnes's son. Do you remember Agnes? She had just come to the village when you left."

The stranger shook his head and Big Dollag continued: "Agnes is not from our village at all. She came from another village. She's an incomer. Don't you remember her?"

The man shook his head again, and ignoring his mother said to Iain: "Come in here, lad, so that I can talk to you. What's your name?"

71

"Iain, sir."

"A very polite boy." The stranger spoke in a peculiar accent that Iain had never heard before and now and again he would swivel his neck nervously as if he were searching for some object that he couldn't see.

"Are you a clever boy? Are you smart? Do you go to school?"

"I go to school, sir," said Iain who felt too embarrassed to admit to being clever. However Dollag, who would at times, surprisingly, hear certain statements as if they were struck like bells through a deep silence, suddenly remarked:

"They say he's clever. They say he's good at his books."

"Good boy, you keep that up. You keep that up, boy."

"Jim's been away in America for twenty years," Dollag shouted joyously. "We never heard from him and then yesterday he knocked on the door. I didn't know him at first. I thought it was a man selling carpets," and she laughed loudly, her belly shaking like a vast jelly, "but it was my own son Jim. You tell your mother that, that Dollag's son is home. You tell her that."

When Iain went home he did tell his mother, as he had been instructed to do, and she said: "Jim's home, is he? Would you credit that now? He's been in America for twenty years or so. They say he was very clever but he had an argument with his father and his father told him to clear off and he did too. He ended up in America. No one knew what the argument was about. It was when I came to this village with your father more than twenty years ago. I was just a bride." And she looked out of the window at the bare landscape as if she expected to see herself by miracle rise from it, in her white bridal gown with a bouquet of flowers in her hand, her husband holding her by the arm.

"Some say the argument was about a girl. He's not married, is he? Is his wife there?"

"I don't know. I only saw him."

"Hm. Anyway, as I was saying, he went off to America. Others

72

said that the argument was about the croft. Jim's the oldest, you see, and his father said that he wouldn't leave him the croft because he didn't show any interest in it. He was a shy boy or so I've heard. And so he's come back again after all these years. That's very funny. Did he look poor?"

"He was wearing a coat and he was sitting by the fire," Iain volunteered, for he was glad to see his mother in such a good humour, and so interested.

"Is that right? Of course their climate is different from ours. He finds it colder here, I suppose. I can see that. Did he come on the bus?"

"I don't know."

"Of course he might have a car. Coming from America he might have a car."

"I didn't see a car," said Iain judiciously. "There might have been one but I didn't see it."

"Well, if you didn't see one," said his mother, laughing, "there can't be one. He wouldn't keep it in the bedroom, would he?" And she continued her ironing.

"I wonder if he's come for good or if he's just on holiday. Maybe he's retired. A lot of them make enough money to retire on but many of them take to drink too when they're out there. What did he say to you? Was he talking to you? He asked you if you were clever? What did you say? I hope you didn't tell him that you were. That would be boasting. Anyway you're only clever in certain things." She put down the iron decisively. "I don't think he's married and I don't think he's done well for himself. That's my opinion." She resumed her ironing, pressing the iron against the white sheet, and added:

"There was a man from our village who came back from America and he spent his time walking about the moors with a stick. He never did a stroke of work but that was because he had retired and had plenty of money."

She didn't say any more and Iain forgot about Jim, Dollag's son, till one day he was rather late in collecting the milk and found that Jim was the only person in the house apart from his brother who was quietly repairing his green net in the usual corner.

"Come in, lad," said Jim. "Tell me, do you read books?"

"Yes," Iain replied shyly.

"Well, then, I'm getting crates of books sent to me from the States and you can read some of them if you like. Would you like that?"

"Yes thank you, sir. Thank you very much."

"Remember that then. Every day you come in here you ask if the crates have come and I'll tell you. Is that OK, lad?"

So every day Iain would ask that question, till one beautiful morning, when the sun was shining and the dew was wet on the grass and the birds were singing, the books did finally come and Iain was allowed to search among them to his heart's content. It was a day he would remember for ever, for among those books he found P. C. Wren stories of the Foreign Legion, a collection of detective stories edited by Dorothy L. Sayers, a massive book of ghost stories, another huge volume of stories about the sea and finally one of spy stories.

Every evening, that enchanted summer, he read those books, firing from forts in a desert glittering under the merciless glare of the sun, duelling with Germans in a dark Prussian forest, investigating cases with Sax Rohmer, sailing tropical seas and lying at anchor in blue lagoons.

And every morning before going to school he would go for the milk and Jim would be sitting by the fire in his coat and saying to him, "How are you getting on, lad? You keep reading."

Was it his imagination or did Jim appear to be getting thinner every day, did his face appear more and more unshaven and shadowed, did he shiver more uncontrollably beside the large fire?

And his mother would say, "He's home for good and everyone says he has no money. He's like the rest of the family, a bit odd. Did you know that he's drinking a lot and that the other night the bus driver had to help him into the house?"

"Shut up," Iain shouted.

"What? What did you say?"

"I didn't say anything."

"You said 'Shut up.' Who do you think you're saying 'shut up' to? Don't speak to me like that."

And Iain muttered something under his breath while his mother glared at him, hands on hips.

Jim said very little to him. He never told him what had happened to him in America, what the cities were like, what criminals haunted the streets, what buildings towered into the sky.

And evening after evening Iain broke complicated codes, made dying confessions about stolen jewellery, hung from the yard arm, travelled through deserts and seas.

One morning Jim wasn't sitting by the fire as he usually was and Dollag told Iain that her son was resting in bed.

"Would you like to go and see him?" she shouted though not with her usual cheerfulness.

"Yes, please," said Iain and he was ushered into a small room with a bed, chair and curtains that had only been partially drawn.

"It's you, boy," said Jim. "Come in. I'll be up soon. It's just that I don't feel so good. How are the books going? OK? When I was your age I read a lot too. Even in the States I read. When you get right down to it, boy, people fail you but books never fail you, and you can take that from me. You remember that." He sat up in bed, wearing a blue cardigan, his face a bluish colour, and continued, "You know something, son. I left home because my father was always telling me 'You give up those books now. You're wasting your time. Why aren't you learning to fish like your brothers? Why aren't you learning to scythe?' In the States though I had some peace." And then he muttered as if to himself, "I should never have come home."

"What did you do in America, sir?" Iain ventured timidly.

"What did I do, eh? Well, I'll tell you. I worked on the elevators, lad, and every night after a hard day's work I would go home to my books. Do you know what elevators are? Well, they're not what you call lifts. They're grain elevators. That's where I worked till I got tired. My boy, America is a terrible place. Don't ever go there. America is the most terrible place on earth." His hollow eyes seemed to stare towards it, that desolate vast country almost too violent and brash for his imagination to encompass. Then he settled back on to his pillow again and said, "Books never fail you, lad, though people will." He didn't say another word, as if he had passed on to Iain the final epigram which contained his whole experience of life, and after a while Iain left the room, almost on tiptoe.

"How is he this morning?" Big Dollag shouted anxiously and Iain replied, 'I don't know."

The jug of milk in his hand he left her house and went home through the singing birds of summer among the flowers which grew all around him.

Two weeks after that his mother told him, after he had come from school, that Jim had died and it seemed to him that there was a certain triumph in her voice.

"He was drinking too much. Everyone was saying that. He killed himself, going up town night after night, and never speaking to anybody. Big Dollag won't like that, the scandal of it. He was just like her other sons, there was a weakness in that family. When I came here first Big Dollag wouldn't speak to me because I was an incomer, and she would say things about your own father —

that he drank too much — but now I'm getting my own back on her. There's a want in her family and everybody knows it," and, thin-lipped, she stared into the bleak world of her triumph.

Iain gazed at her horrified as if he knew that of all the people whom he had met in the village Jim had been the one who had been most like himself, quiet, withdrawn, imaginative. He ran out of the room and climbed into the attic where his books were. Weeping he took them out, thinking about Jim but not as if Jim were dead, for he was too young to imagine what death was.

Then he began to read "Beau Geste" by P. C. Wren and was soon lost in the desert again with the Foreign Legion, having forgotten his mother's petty words; Big Dollag; the village, bare and unharmonious below him; and was himself, in spite of everything, true and upright and honourable in a fortress in the desert almost devoid of humanity and beaten upon by a torrid sun. And it seemed to him as if Jim was there also, standing beside him, his rifle at his shoulder, wearing a pill-box hat, while the tribes attacked, appearing over the horizon in undisciplined but venomous hordes.

13

"I WANT TO go for a walk to the sea," said Pauline, tiring of sailing paper boats on the small pond.

"All right," said Iain.

Pauline was the daughter of a lady who came from London to the village every year during the summer holidays and who in fact belonged to the village though she was now married in the metropolis. Most of the villagers were polite to her, but behind her back they said that she put on airs and adopted a condescending manner to them as if they were peasants who had seen nothing of the world. She dressed in a green costume, and always carried a handbag ("even to the byre," some of them said, meaning of course the lavatory, since none of the houses had toilets or even water of their own), and spoke as if there were marbles in her mouth. One would have thought from her conversation, they said, that she knew the Queen well, that she regularly bought her jewellery in Bond Street, attended a doctor in Harley Street, and was regarded with reverence when she appeared at Horse Guards Parade. In actual fact, as far as could be ascertained, her husband worked as a clerk, was a small hunted-looking man with sleeked hair and shiny suits who never was heard to speak in his wife's presence, and, when he did speak, conversed in an extraordinary form of English that no one in the village understood. Iain, however, was allowed to play with Pauline who was eleven years old like himself, wore ribbons in her blond pigtails and unlike many of the village children seemed preternaturally well dressed and clean: on this particular occasion she wore pink stockings and a pink dress.

As they walked down the path between the cornfields, Iain now and again kicking moodily at a stone, Pauline was thinking of the expedition as a great adventure. It was only after she had been chattering on for some time that Iain realised that she had never been at the sea before, though she mentioned that she had been on a boat on the river Thames. He found it quite extraordinary that anybody could have lived in a place which was not near the sea and desperately tried to visualise London.

"Is it bigger than Stornoway?" he asked.

"It's so big that you can get lost in it," Pauline replied, completely disdaining the reference to Stornoway. "I got lost in it," she added proudly. "One day when Mummy was in a shop I got lost and a policeman had to take me home."

"Was it Scotland Yard?" Iain asked.

"No, of course not. It was a policeman with a helmet." She said this decisively as if it settled the truth of her story once and for all. "He was very tall and he had a helmet," she repeated for good measure.

"What do you call this lovely lovely flower?" she asked, staring down at a yellow plant that grew in the field.

"I don't know. Is there no water in London then?"

"I told you. There's the river Thames. I told you that before."

"Oh?" Iain gave up trying to visualise London and told her, "When we get to the bottom we go through a gate and then we walk to the sea."

"Is it much bigger than the Thames then?"

"Rivers are fresh water, you know," said Iain expansively. "The sea is salt. That's the difference between the sea and a river."

"Salt. How does it get salt?"

"I don't know but it is. Maybe the salt was in from the

beginning for thousands and thousands of years. The clouds drop their rain on it all the time."

When they arrived at the gate Iain had to open it for her, because she didn't understand how the bolt worked, and she wasn't strong enough to pull the gate back. Her shoes had blades of wet grass on them, and even her socks were wet from walking through the high wet plants; she stopped to wipe her shoes clean and then followed Iain who had gone on ahead, proud of the fact that he was the leader, that he knew where he was going, and that under no circumstances would he get lost.

They walked along the road to the sea, passing cows on the way who stared loweringly at them, and then turned their heads away as if they were tired of the sight.

When they arrived at the beach, Pauline gazed at the vast glittering expanse of sea in astonishment:

"Is that all water?" she asked.

"Of course it is. You can get drowned there. Some boys were drowned in a boat there."

"In a boat?"

"Not in the boat. When they were out in the boat. See. That's what you call seaweed."

"It's like long ribbons. Long brown ribbons. Do you think I could take some back to show Mummy?"

"No, it's too dirty. Come on. We might find a crab. Have you ever seen a crab?"

"Not alive. Where can we get a crab?"

"There may be one in the pool. Not all the time but sometimes. And you can get whelks on the rocks."

Pauline daintily picked her way among the rocks, making sure that her shoes didn't get wet and clutching her skirt as if she were a ballerina.

"There are the boats there," said Iain. "See. There are the oars."

"What are oars?"

"They're for rowing the boat. Don't you know anything?"

"I know lots of things. Do you know who Madame Curie was?"

"Of course I do. She invented radium."

"All right, so you know. You don't need to boast."

"I wasn't boasting. I was telling you."

"I knew already anyway. It's not my fault I don't know about oars. I bet you don't know about subways. I bet you've never been in a subway. I was in a subway lots of times. You go up and down an escalator." She paused for a moment as if wondering whether she had said the word right but in any case Iain wasn't listening to her for he had seen a crab.

"See," he said, "you can touch it. It's a big crab. Don't let it nip you."

"Nip you?" she said enquiringly.

"Bite you with its claws," replied Iain despairingly. One would think someone who had come from London would at least know the English language.

Pauline touched the crab reverently and gently and it moved a little through the water under her hand.

"I wonder what it's thinking about," she said. "I wonder what crabs think about."

"I don't know," said Iain impatiently. "You were lucky to see a crab. You don't find them here all the time. Look, there's a jelly fish."

"Just like an umbrella," said Pauline delightedly. "It's like a tiny umbrella." She touched it very lightly with her finger and then followed Iain who was standing among some rocks.

"Here are the whelks," Iain instructed her as if he were a teacher. "They stick to the rocks but you can pull them away. See. Inside it, there's the meat. We take it out with a pin and then we boil it in a pot."

"Is the meat good? Is it not very salty?"

"It's not salty. Out there, do you see, there's a ship. It's a liner. Do you see it sailing past? That island has got sheep on it."

"How do they get out there? Do they swim?"

"Of course they don't. People take them out and leave them there. Sheep don't swim." At least he thought they didn't swim, though perhaps one or two might: dogs certainly could swim.

"Maybe," said Pauline, "their wool would pull them down into the water. Maybe they would drown," said Pauline seriously. "Maybe that's what would happen."

And then, "Can we not go over there," pointing to the stone quay.

"If you like," said Iain airily though he didn't want to go.

"We were at the fish market," said Pauline suddenly. "It's called Billinsgate, I think, and we were at Madame Tussauds. They've got statues of murderers and they've got axes and knives with blood on them and it's very dark. And they've got chains and pots."

They walked over to the stone quay, which was deserted, though sometimes there would be boys fishing with bait for cuddies, dangling their legs over the edge. Iain was glad that there was no one there, for he didn't want to be seen with a girl, especially one from London who had never seen the sea before, and who wore pigtails as well. He would never live it down. He was angry with himself that he hadn't thought of the boys before and had agreed so thoughtlessly to come down to the sea. It just showed one that one must remember things like that.

When they reached the quay, Pauline stood at the very edge to peer down into the water and Iain called her back.

"If you go too near the edge you'll fall," he said, and for a moment he had a vision of her small body with the pink frock and the blond pigtails floating eerily among the stones.

"Look," said Pauline, "I can see more seaweed and stones. The water's green here. It's beautiful."

"It's blue further out," Iain told her. "That's because it's deeper."

Suddenly Pauline turned away from the edge and began to jump over the capstans which were sunk into the stone of the quay, three or four of them, made of iron.

"You do that, Iain," she shouted; "you jump too." At first he didn't want to, because the capstans were so near the edge, but he knew that he must jump because she had and he jumped too, following her little figure over capstan after capstan.

After a while she grew tired of this and sat down on one of them. "What are you going to do when you grow up?" she asked Iain.

"I don't know. I might be a writer."

"I'm going to be a nurse and cure people. I'm going to work in a hospital. I saw little fish there just now."

"Where?"

"Just there. There."

"I can't see any. I'm going to write about the Foreign Legion."

"What's that, Iain? Do you see it? It's a ladder."

Iain pretended not to notice it. "Where?"

"There. Just below. I dare you to climb down the ladder."

"I don't want to. Anyway we should be going home."

"No, not yet. I want to climb down the ladder."

"It's too dangerous. You would fall into the water."

"I've climbed a ladder before. It was in a big empty house we found. And we saw this ladder and I and another girl climbed it."

"I won't let you. It's too dangerous."

"You can't stop me."

"I will stop you."

"You're scared, that's what you are. Scaredy, scaredy."

"I'm not."

"You are."

"Not."

"Are."

"Not."

"Are."

Iain stood on the stone quay while she taunted him and it seemed to him strange that she should have found out so soon what he was most scared of, and at the same time he knew that he would have to climb down the ladder because she was a girl and he was a boy. He walked over to where the ladder was and as he stood above it he felt it as a snake that was ready to flash out at him with its fangs. Pauline was now sitting on the capstan again dangling her legs and watching him, her face small and pretty and cruel.

"All right," he said and knelt down on the quay feeling for the first rung of the ladder, his hand grasping the iron bar sunk in the stone of the quay.

His leg felt and felt for the first rung, and his breath was short, for there seemed to be a constriction in his chest, and there was sweat on his brow. He found it and clutching the iron bar as if with a death grip he let his foot stand on the first rung. Then it was the second rung and he was still holding the bar which he would soon have to let go. Below him was the water and the stones but he did not dare look and he had forgotten about Pauline and all he could see was the dented wet stone in front of his face. He felt for the third rung and the fourth rung and then he moved his right hand away from the iron bar while still clutching it with his left. Then his right hand had grasped the top rung and now his left hand had gripped it. As he descended slowly, still not looking down, he felt his foot slip on the rung below, for it was smooth with seaweed, and for a moment he thought he was going to fall as he slithered hither and thither, checking the scream from his throat, and trembling violently. He could hear no sound from above him as if Pauline had also forgotten about him, and disdained even to follow his progress.

Below him was the sea and the stones and the seaweed and his sandals were sliding along the rungs, not getting a proper grip, and his hands grasped the rungs as if they would never let go. Steadily, steadily he descended, cursing his sandals and wishing that he had worn proper boots, slithering, sliding, his arms sore, his teeth biting his lips. Then he had reached the last rung and he was safe below among the shallow water and the stones.

And at that moment he was filled with such joy as he had never felt before in his life, so that he danced among the shallow water and the stones like a Red Indian, and gazing at the iron ladder which now seemed so harmless he shook his fist at it. "I've done it, I've done it," he shouted. Then above him he could see Pauline looking down as if she were a princess in a tower and he shouted to her, "Don't come down, I'll come up. The ladder is all slippery. There's seaweed on it."

He ran splashing through the water and arrived at where she was standing on the stone quay, small and pink in her dress, her pigtails about her head, her red lips parted.

"I didn't want you to go," she was saying and she was almost crying, as she looked at his drenched sandals.

"It's all right," he replied grandly. "I wanted to go. It's not too difficult."

She came up to him and put her hand in his and he ran away embarrassed, while she ran after him. He thought he could do anything: he could climb down that old ladder any time now. He raced down the road at full speed, Pauline less quickly running after him, and then after a while he slowed down and waited for her. After all if it hadn't been for her he wouldn't have gone down the ladder at all and it would have remained forever in his mind as something that had defeated him. Her pigtails flying, she was shouting something to him that he couldn't understand.

He was older than her so he had to wait: at least he felt older than her now, older and calmer and wiser. It was as if she were his younger sister, though she was just as old as him, and much more ignorant since she had never seen the sea before and didn't know anything about crabs and whelks and things like that. Her eyes turned down shyly to the ground when she reached him as if she had sensed the change in their relationship and were acknowledging his superiority and that was, he thought, as it should be.

All the way home she only answered when he spoke and he didn't speak much for he didn't feel the need for speaking. It was as if by climbing down the ladder he had entered deeper and calmer waters than he had known. It was only much later that he felt a great sadness as if by climbing the ladder he had taken away from

86

himself a challenge that would never now be a challenge again. But by that time Pauline was in London, miles and miles away, among her subways and her Madame Tussauds, and she soon faded from his mind altogether, though in later years he would remember her with gratitude and sorrow. In fact, he never saw her again in his whole life.

14

IT WAS CHRISTMAS Day and there was a light fall of snow on the ground that had drifted there during the night. Having received his present, a toy car which ran along the green linoleum when it was wound up, Iain went outside into the day which was illuminated by a red sun low on the horizon which seemed to cast a reddish shade across the snow. He saw a crow rocking slightly on a fence, and a buzzard wheeling about the reddish sky.

He wasn't going anywhere in particular and it was near a small pool of frozen water that he saw the shoe. It was lying beside the pool and a little snow had drifted over it. For some reason, Iain stopped and flicked the snow away from the shoe, which he held lightly in his hand. It was an old black shoe, wrinkled and laceless, and the heel was almost worn away. Iain held it up against the sun thinking of nothing and now and again examining the leather and wondering whose shoe it had been. It was definitely not a woman's shoe or a girl's shoe and from its size it seemed to be more a man's shoe than a boy's. It had received much use in its time, he thought, for not only was the heel worn away but there were many nails missing from the sole.

He looked all round him but could see nothing else lying on the ground apart from the shoe, which seemed very ancient in comparison with his own. When the pool was unfrozen he would sail his paper boat with its paper sail on it, but now it was iced over and instead of the boat there was this shoe. He turned it over and over in his hand as if he were trying to question it. It reminded him of the soppy compositions that Miss Stilton would make them write on their black slates, "A Day in the Life of a Postage Stamp" or "A Day in the Life of a Penny". . . . A Day in the Life of a Shoe. He put his hand inside it and felt a nail or a stud protruding and it made him think of the village cobbler who would sit outside his door in the summer months repairing shoes for the villagers, the hammer in his hand, the nails in his mouth, the light falling on the round bald head which looked exactly like a naked stone. He sucked his finger where the nail had bitten him.

A shoe on Christmas Day. Something in the words stirred his mind as if they were trying to send him a message. But what could the shoe have to do with Christmas, with the parcels that had come down the chimney and lay on the table in the chill bare morning, as over the cold linoleum he himself barefootedly and excitedly moved. What could the shoe have to do with Christmas, with the angels and the stars and the baby, especially with the stars that shone so brightly in the sky as they did above his own village on a winter night. Nothing that he could see. And yet here he was bent down on the chill ground holding this old shoe in his hand reddened by the cold.

His mind as if conscious of the snow and the red light around him roved among pictures: of the Eskimos swathed in their heavy furs making holes in the ice and patiently fishing; of Russians in sleighs racing across the steppes under a low sky; of the wind flapping a flag at the North Pole; of icebergs floating like ghosts across the vast Atlantic Ocean. Those pictures had all come from the green-covered geography book which Miss Stilton had recently given them.

His hand holding the shoe was cold and he laid the shoe down on the frozen pool and watched it as if at any moment it would start to move. But the shoe stayed where it was, frayed, wrinkled, ancient, laceless. Iain thought that he ought to go back to his house and play some more with the red car but he didn't really want to, for he didn't like the car much, though he appreciated the gift.

After all, once one had wound it up a few times and let it run across the green linoleum, there was nothing much else that one could expect from it. It would just do the same thing again and again and again, for that was all it could do.

He raised his head and looked at the village which lay absolutely still under the reddish light. The people were warm in their houses but the shoe was out here in the cold day exposed and chill and warped. Why was there only one shoe? It seemed so lonely without its companion. Where then was the other one? One lonely shoe out on the grass beside a frosty pond under the gloomy light. It was, however, as if the light, raw and lowering, were trying to tell him something about the shoe. But that was ridiculous. What could the light tell him? About anything? And why was he kneeling in this ridiculous fashion on the icy ground? If anyone were to see him they would think him stupid. But he didn't get to his feet just the same.

Pictures of Christmas came into his mind, and one in particular of the Virgin Mary bending over Jesus in the manger while the dumb animals looked over her shoulder, as if they were trying to see him. But of course the animals didn't know anything about what was happening and neither apparently did the innkeeper, for he had kept them outside the door of the noisy inn. And that was terrible, especially after they had ridden for such a long distance. On an ass. He saw them quite clearly in the raw light, bowed and dispirited, standing at the door in their long dusty clothes, wearing their dusty sandals.

He knelt there, the shoe in his hand, as if he were listening at a shut door. And as he listened it seemed to him as if the hand containing the shoe began to tremble, not with the cold but with something else, with the message. He looked down at the shoe and both it and his hand were shaking, vibrating. What an extraordinary thing. And yet he wasn't frightened at all, it was rather as if he was overwhelmed with joy. It was as if the whole village began to vibrate, all the houses, all the walls, all the fences, and then he saw the black shoe under a red sky and the shoe itself was turning a shade of red in his hand, while in the distance, once, clearly, he heard the crowing of a cock.

He gazed around him and it was as if he heard music, and as well as that it was as if his body was full of water like the buckets that he would carry home from the well, brimming over. The cottages and landscape had turned into a village such as he imagined might exist in Finland or Russia, and at any moment he expected sleighs to come rushing towards him, bearing old bearded men who were wearing old wrinkled shoes such as he held in his hand. And they all had the face of the Cook or the cobbler. As they approached the village the houses trembled and shook as if in the red water that had appeared in front of them. The water was mounting his body and reaching his head which was warming steadily while the shoe still shook in his hand, more violently than ever.

He gazed directly into the sun as he knelt on the ground, the shoe in his hand, and more clearly he heard the music which was outside and inside him at the same time, and it was very loud as if it were a song of praise that was arising from the reddish-white ground all around him. At the centre of it all was the old shoe, wrinkled and helpless, and yet not ashamed among the music. The shoe, the shoe, his mind or something else that was not his mind kept muttering over and over, it is to do with the shoe. To do with the shoe, to do with the shoe. The shoe is not new, the shoe is old. Bold. Rolled. Scold. Sold. Told. The chains of words hung before him like a long ladder in the cold red raw light.

His body was full to bursting as if some joy was trying to get out, to run and run and then say something, speak. His hand holding the shoe trembled but not so violently as before. He must get home, he must get paper, there was something he should put down lest it should spill. It was something to do with the shoe, the frozen pond, the red sky, sleighs, silent houses, white roads. It was something to do with all that, but what exactly? Shoe, true, blue, flew . . . The crow rested lightly on the fence, its feathers aflame, the buzzard hovered in the sky, and the black shoe trembled in his hand.

He laid it down on the ground and then he began to run, and he burst into the house and climbed the door into the attic where he kept the paper and pencil with which on wet days he drew his endless drifters and motor boats. It was as if he must hurry before the water spilt, before the buckets were empty. With his pencil in his hand, he gazed out over his territory, through the skylight, his hand ready to race over the paper, not knowing what he was writing, with such speed, never before with such speed, never before with such joy, lest anyone should come, lest Kenneth should come with his barbaric cries.

The red sun stared back at him with its raw eye between the two hills. In its light he wrote, in its cold wintry light.

15

"I WANT YOU to go and ask Mrs Macdonald if you can borrow half a crown till I get my pension next Tuesday," said his mother to Iain one day.

"I don't want to go," said Iain angrily. "Kenneth can go this time. It's his turn. I went two weeks ago."

"Not me," said Kenneth, grinning provocatively.

"Why not you?"

"I don't want to go, that's all. You go."

"Yes, Iain, you go. Kenneth is no good at these things." Across her face passed a spasm of what might have been rage or shame.

"Why are we always having to borrow money?" Iain pursued, still angry at the unfairness of Kenneth's refusal.

"Because . . . It's not your business. You do what you're told."

Kenneth made faces at him across the table when his mother was not looking and Iain banged down his book.

"Stop that at once and do what you're told," his mother shouted, her face white with rage, her bluish lips compressed.

"It's unfair," Iain muttered. "Kenneth never goes. And anyway . . ."

"Anyway what?"

"We're the only ones who borrow money. Nobody else borrows money. I hate it."

"There's nothing wrong with borrowing. She will get her money back, never fear. There's not one of them that I can't face. There was a day when I didn't have to do it but I have to do it now. Tell her she will get it back on Tuesday. Now run."

Iain turned away from his grimacing brother and his inflexible mother, fuming and trembling. If there was one thing he hated above all it was going to someone's house to borrow money. Why were they so poor that they never had any money? He swore that when he grew up he would make sure he was rich and never have to ask anyone for half a crown or even a single penny.

Kicking at the stones on the road, he walked across to Mrs Macdonald's house and hoped above all things that she would be alone so that he could get the half-crown and run back home again to continue reading his book. He wished Kenneth would drop dead: sometimes he hated him with a bitter hatred. He was never asked to do anything, all because his mother said that he, Iain, was better at these things. Well, he wasn't. And anyway why couldn't his mother go herself? She was nearer to Mrs Macdonald's age than he was.

Thinking these thoughts, and bitterly angry and resentful, he arrived at Mrs Macdonald's house and stood there for a while, reluctant to go in, watching the door which seemed inhospitable and was certainly and blankly shut. He didn't like Mrs Macdonald but she had been chosen because his mother had gone the rounds of most of the other people in the village who would be likely to lend her money, and only Mrs Macdonald remained. She was a thin woman in black who crept about the houses and always had a drip from her nose and a habit of calling him "a ghraidh" which he hated because he knew she didn't mean it and it also made him feel like a girl.

He waited, undecided at her door, wishing he could kick it or that he could run away somewhere, anywhere, where people didn't have to borrow money and where there were no Mrs Macdonalds and no Kenneths who got away with doing nothing.

Then gritting his teeth he walked into the house, not knocking on the door, and there she was sitting by the fire but not, to his consternation, alone, for with her was Mrs Murray and they were

both drinking tea: or at least they had tea cups and plates on a little stool between them.

Flushed with shame and tongue-tied, he stood at the door of the living room not knowing what to say, for he couldn't bring himself to ask Mrs Macdonald for money while there was another woman with her.

"Come in," said Mrs Macdonald with surprise, "come in," and she looked meaningfully at Mrs Murray. "We haven't seen you for a long time. Come in and sit down."

He pushed his way as if through water to the chair, pretending that he had come to visit, while he felt that even his legs and knees were blushing and that if he looked at them he would see spreading all over them a bright glaring red. He had no idea what to say and wished that the house would fall on all three of them, burying them in rubble and dust.

"This is Agnes's boy," said Mrs Macdonald to Mrs Murray, as if Mrs Murray didn't know and again he sensed the secret look they gave each other.

"I know that," said Mrs Murray, whom he didn't like either and who was the wife of fat Donald who didn't do any work but spent his days complaining about his back and showing his injured wrist to anyone who was interested.

"I know that," Mrs Murray repeated. "Agnes's boy." And her heavy malicious eyes seemed to encompass him without actually looking.

He sat down in the immense silence inside which there crawled worms of shame which he could feel climbing his legs to his knees and nibbling hotly.

"And have you any news for us, a ghraidh?" Mrs Macdonald asked, turning her thin beaky face towards him.

"I haven't heard anything," Iain muttered, looking down at his sandals.

"He hasn't heard anything," said Mrs Macdonald to Mrs Murray as if she were deaf and couldn't hear the answer.

"Nothing?" said Mrs Murray as if she felt astonished.

"Would you like a biscuit?" Mrs Macdonald asked him, smiling the sort of smile which she considered suitable for a boy, ingratiating and benevolent.

"No thank you. I . . ." And at that moment he nearly asked her for the half-crown before he had settled into his seat, while he was still able to rush out of the house, while Mrs Macdonald was not as yet prepared. But the moment passed and he didn't ask, and as if he weren't there at all Mrs Murray said to her friend, apparently continuing an earlier tale:

"So that's what she gave him for his tea then, herring and treacle. Did you ever hear the like?"

"Never," said Mrs Macdonald. "Never. If she had even given him potatoes. Or scones. But herring and treacle. No wonder the poor man is complaining about his stomach. Who would wonder?"

"You're right enough. This is a nice biscuit you have here. Did you get it in the shop?"

"No, not in the shop. I was up town yesterday."

"Did you see anyone?"

"No. I wasn't long up. Oh, I'm telling a lie. I was speaking to John Munro. He's looking very white. Is it TB, do you think?"

"They say that but we don't know. He would have been at the doctor," and she leaned forward, speaking in a whisper as if to make sure that Iain didn't hear her. "Everyone knows, you understand, but . . ." And she nodded her head with great significance as did Mrs Macdonald, so that as they moved their heads in unison they looked like two dolls.

Iain sitting on his chair could hear the clock ticking very loudly. He gazed intently at a picture on the wall which showed two ducks with necks outstretched flying through a pale sky. He gazed and gazed at it as if it were the most interesting picture in the world so that if anyone happened to look at him they would know that he was occupied with every detail of the painting and that he would have no time to answer their questions. He held his breath so that the women wouldn't even notice that he was there, and pulled his legs towards him, locking them firmly round the legs of the chair. The time for speaking had passed and now he would have to wait till after a while he could decently go.

"Things are dear in the town," Mrs Macdonald was now saying. "I saw a hat but I didn't buy it, it was so dear."

"You're right," said Mrs Murray, "you're right. I can't afford to go myself as you know but I'm sure the hats are dear." Her voice had a whining self-pitying quality as if she suffered a lot of grief which very few people knew about except herself.

"It was in Ritchie's I saw it. A black hat with a veil on it. It was going to cost one pound and two shillings but I didn't buy it." She sighed heavily.

"And the girls in the shops are so rude, they say," remarked Mrs Murray, "they say that they're so rude. Some of them from our own village too, mentioning no names," and she glanced at Iain as if she had said too much.

Iain was still staring at the painting, diminishing himself to a spot on the chair, to a mote in the room. Why did Mrs Macdonald have money and his mother not? Why did she have ornaments and a beautiful clock? And yet she was uglier than his mother, and he hated her. Why am I here, he thought, why can't I just go? But he couldn't bring himself to do so for his body seemed to be made of stone, while at the same time it trembled with shame. In the picture the ducks flew on their undeviating way towards the warmer climates.

As if she had just remembered him Mrs Macdonald asked, "And how is your mother, a ghraidh?"

"She's all right, thank you."

"That's good, that's good," said Mrs Macdonald, giving the same meaningful look to Mrs Murray as before.

"Yes, health is the best thing we have," Mrs Murray remarked largely. "What are we without our health?"

"What indeed? We can have money but if we don't have our health we have nothing."

"That's very true," sighed Mrs Murray. "You never said a truer word. You could have all the money in the world and if you didn't have your health you'd have nothing."

There was another long silence while the two women stared into the fire and Iain gazed at the painting on the wall.

"I've just heard," began Mrs Murray, "I've just heard . . ."

And at that moment, at that very moment, at that moment trembling with nervousness, Iain got to his feet and without doing anything more than muttering, "I've got to go," he made a supreme effort and trudged as if through some substance like porridge or treacle to the door which seemed indeed to be miles away.

"Thank you for your visit, a ghraidh," said Mrs Macdonald with her ingratiating smile, "and tell your mother I was asking for her."

"And me too," said Mrs Murray.

Then he was out in the fresh air, the door shut behind him. Of couse he couldn't have asked for money while Mrs Murray was there. It would have been all over the village in minutes. Even his mother could see that. Anyone could see that. He looked down at his empty hands and then at the quiet village and finally at his own house where his mother – and Kenneth – would be waiting, expecting him to come home with the money. His mother would be angry, she might even hit him: her rages were terrible because she was poor and had no money and also she was exceedingly proud. Some day he would get money for her, some day he would be rich and give her so much money that she would never need to borrow again. He swore that as if to the red sun that was setting directly ahead of him.

"You should have waited," she would say to him, "you should have waited till Mrs Murray left. That's what you should have done." But how could he have waited? Mrs Murray might not have left for hours and how could his mother know what it was like to sit in that chair, in silence, having nothing to contribute to the conversation, while the two women talked to each other mysteriously as if he wasn't there. He would rather starve. He would rather not have bread or tea or soup than do that. He would rather go hungry, though indeed he was hungry at that moment.

He walked back very slowly, looking down at the ground all the time, now and again stopping to see what was in the ditch and even hoping that by some miracle he would find a half-crown lying on the road. But he knew that such a miracle wouldn't happen, no miracles ever came his way: they were more likely to happen to Kenneth than to him. He would have to invent a story, that Mrs Macdonald wasn't in, that's what he must say. And he knew that if he said it his mother would send him somewhere else, to some other house where people were at home. And at that moment as he gazed across the slightly frosted landscape with the red sun ahead of him it reminded him of the picture with the two ducks, their necks outstretched, flying towards the sun, while below them were the marshes: below them in their turn were Mrs Macdonald and Mrs Murray sitting by the fire eating their biscuits.

He remembered the last time he had returned empty-handed, the expression on his mother's face of whiteness and fear, as if she were gazing and not for the first time into a deep terrible pit. So he stood there by the empty ditch, perplexed and afraid, while in the distance he could see the sun, raw and red like a burning coin at the far end of the landscape, his heart, as he watched, torn with shame and rage, on that cold empty wintry afternoon.

16

THE SMALL GREY-HAIRED precise man walked up the path to the house while Iain's mother was hanging up sheets on the line in a fresh spring breeze that whipped them about her face. She recognised him through a lash of white as the headmaster of the little village school which she herself had attended long ago under a different and more unpredictably raging predecessor, and which Iain and Kenneth were attending now. He stood smiling on the pathway near the house till she had finished fixing the sheets to the line and then noticing that she was flurried and nervous and trying to dry her hands on her long skirt, he said, "It's nothing to do with misbehaviour on the part of Iain or Kenneth, Mrs Campbell. Nothing at all. I can assure you of that."

His trim head and body assured her of that most surely, but she stood where she was, afraid to ask him in in case he thought her house untidy, and at the same time frightened that he would consider her inhospitable. He finally solved the problem by inviting himself in.

"Please," he said and pointed to a chair. She sat down, her hands folded in her lap, and he did the same.

"As a matter of fact," he began, "I came about Iain."

"What is it about Iain that the headmaster wants to know," she asked, hoping that he hadn't noticed the patch on the curtains, or the worn linoleum.

"Well, as a matter of fact it's nothing serious. I've been watching Iain for some time now. Indeed he studies Latin with me and I've noticed that he has a real love of learning. He reads a lot, doesn't he?"

"He never takes his head out of a book," said Mrs Campbell, as if a book were a trough. "He even reads at the peat bank." The headmaster permitted himself a little smile as at a joke completely understood, for by it Mrs Campbell was implying that to Iain books were more important than the tasks of the day.

"I can believe that, Mrs Campbell, I can well believe that." The curtains were astir with the spring breeze, and she thought that surely he must notice now, but all he said was, "It's fine spring weather we're having, Mrs Campbell. I saw some lambs today for the first time." They say that if the first lamb is looking directly towards you you will have good luck, Mrs Campbell thought irrelevantly, as she turned her slightly lowered gaze in the direction of the headmaster in his well-cut precise grey suit and his polished black shoes.

"To put it in a nutshell, Mrs Campbell, what I would want to happen would be that Iain should attend the big secondary school in the town this autumn. Now before you say anything," and he raised his white hand, "it won't cost you anything. He will get a bursary – at least I am almost certain he will – and that will pay for his bus fare. I think that he is" – and he paused impressively – "university material."

Her mind tried to grapple with what the headmaster was saying. Material? What material? If only the man could speak Gaelic she would find it easier to understand; but no, he spoke English, though she must admit that his words though mysterious were clearly enunciated.

"You see," the headmaster continued, as if he were lecturing, "there are few in this village of whom it can be said that they are university material," (so it was a favourable thing then, was it?) "and therefore we must strike while the iron is hot. We must take measures in good time."

Finally she came to his meaning as a bird circling fearfully finally settles on a branch.

"Is the headmaster saying that Iain could go to university?"

"That is precisely what I am saying, Mrs Campbell. In my opinion his grasp, particularly of languages — though he is not so strong on the side of the sciences — is such that I would commit myself to saying that. His quickness in seeing concepts in Latin, his essays and his general knowledge suggest to me that he would make, eventually, a university candidate. Now, Mrs Campbell, the question is do you want him to go to the secondary school? There might be, I can appreciate," and he coughed slightly, "economic barriers in the way." And he looked round the room, from the wooden dresser, with the dishes stacked in tiers on it, to the wooden table with the oilcloth cover.

Mrs Campbell sat stunned in her seat. She had been hoping that in a few years, not very long now, Iain would be able to earn money and she would be forever free of having to borrow a shilling here and a half-crown there: she would be able to go to bed at night knowing where the morrow's meals would come from, she would be, in short, like all her neighbours.

"Well, Mrs Campbell?" His voice came to her as if from a far hollow distance, as if he were indeed the evil one tempting her with gifts, placing before her an intolerable choice. For if Iain went to university her days of scrimping would be prolonged, she would be condemned to wear, as far ahead as she could see, even to church, the worn clothes that she already had, there would be no prospect of furniture for the house, she would stare bleakly into a future of continued borrowing, of worry and of toil. And she stayed silent, gazing at a point slightly below the headmaster's chin, bowed and weary.

He continued, however. "The fact is, Mrs Campbell, I know that this will mean hardship for you and that he won't earn money for some years. I can appreciate that side of it but on the other hand if one considers his welfare – his welfare as a whole – then this indubitably is the best thing for him. After all many boys take jobs that lead to nothing."

How fine his language, was. How well he could arrange everything. If only she could do the same. Did he who was talking so glibly about money not realise that money meant butter, bread, sugar, fish, meat, and that lack of money meant an empty larder, and sleepless nights? Would his Latin feed an empty belly or put flesh on growing bones? She stared past him into the years that might come, a continuation of the years that had passed. It wasn't that she thought about Iain's future, for she knew very well that in university he might go astray, he might forget all about her and his own brother, he might never visit them again, and spend his life among corruption.

"Mrs Campbell . . ." She jerked back to reality as he continued, "I do understand the difficulties there will be for you. But I assure you that there will be no problem in the immediate future since as I have said he can pay his bus fares with his bursary. And think also of the honour to the school."

So that was what he was thinking about, the honour to the school. He wasn't thinking of Iain at all, he was thinking of the praise he would receive as one who successfully prepared pupils for the university. Well, Iain was her own flesh and blood and she would show him that she could at least say no if she wished and the "No" came to her lips like meat.

But before she could say it, he added, "There is no question but that Iain is one of the ablest pupils I have had. His imagination is strong and he should go far. I haven't spoken to him about this but I am sure that he himself feels that the possibility is there. The boys of the village won't like it. They never like it when someone leaves them for a higher position and that too is understandable. Still I am sure Iain has enough common sense and tact to take that in his stride. May I therefore take it that you will allow him to go to the secondary school this August?"

He waited and her head whirled. She found it difficult to say "No" directly to the headmaster, though she would easily have said it to anyone in the village. But she would say it. What right had he, moneyed as he was, to come along to her house and take away from her her only hope of a decent future? How could he know anything about poverty, true real grinding poverty? She would send him back to his school first.

And then just as she was about to speak, to let her mouth bang down on the words as the mousetrap on the mouse among the flour, she heard as if very faintly two words that he had used and she clutched at them as a sailor might clutch at a log of wood in a stormy sea: "Higher position." The two words danced enticingly towards her. "Higher position." They were smiling at her. "The boys of the village won't like it." They were happy and smiling and laughing.

"Higher position." She saw Iain, daringly, as a minister, dressed in his minister's gown, ascending into the pulpit and he was castigating all the villagers for their lack of charity, he was telling them about the widow and the widow's mite, he was asking them why they had not, even once, gone to his mother to ask if she needed anything, he was haranguing them for their lack of love. And she imagined their faces twisted with shame and embarrassment as hers had often been, and she herself sitting triumphantly in the front seat looking up at her son, who was transfigured as if by the light of heaven. And she turned her face like iron directly to the headmaster and she said, "Iain shall go to the university."

A remarkable woman, thought the headmaster, as he made his way down the path to the main road, and saw between curtains people peering at him. Not many of the villagers would have put love of scholarship, academic prowess, above indigence and poverty. Not many of them would have had that sort of vision.

So it was that on that spring day he inhaled the fresh invigorating air, and felt within himself the surge and sparkle of salt breezes as he saw the lambs suckling their mothers, the vernal greenness of the grass, and the white road that led back to his own school, where after all his endeavours had not been in vain. So must once the Roman poets have felt at the dawning of their language, alive and happy, setting out past their limiting geographical boundaries into the open sea. So too must Mrs Campbell feel, having made her sacrifice, having transcended her narrow parochial world. And he rejoiced, for he was a good man, and he wanted Iain to do well and on that day he felt virtue and joy all around him as he returned schoolward.

17

WITH THE EMPTY jam jar in his hand Iain set out across the moor, in search of blaeberries, his body bent down to the earth. The moor stretched away from the back of the house and rose in a series of braes past the Standing Stones. Kneeling among the heather he gathered the blaeberries and put them in the jar, steadily making his way further and further from the houses while all about him flew little flies with trembling almost transparent wings, and striped wasps buzzed past his nose. Some of the blaeberries he ate, but most he placed in the jar; and while searching for them he found a lark's abandoned nest, empty of eggs or nestlings, for it was now autumn. When he looked back after a while he found that he had gone over the summit of the brae as a ship goes over the horizon and that he could no longer see the village at all except that he could distinguish trembling stems of greyish-blue smoke ascending into the sky.

All around him were the scarred peat banks, dry and black, with here and there flaky peats that had been left lying and not taken to the houses. To his right he could see the houses of the neighbouring village which curved round one edge of the moor. About him was an immense silence and he could see no one at all moving anywhere near him. For a moment he thought of returning lest he should get lost in the spaces of the moor, but some daring instinct, some sense of adventure, was urging him onwards from the houses anchored to their familiar earth. It was as if he was Columbus setting off into a new world with inadequate maps, charts that showed only dimly and tentatively unknown seas and unknown islands.

The jar was steadily filling and in his absorption it was only now and again that he looked about him. He could no longer see any houses, for he seemed to have climbed another brae. He couldn't even see the Standing Stones. He was in a landscape of broken peat banks, stones and earth, while above him now and again black birds flew, their wings lazily outspread. Steadily he made his way forward, bearing his jar, slightly nervous, slightly excited, seeing no sign of people or of animals. How alone he was, how quiet the world. It was as if he had dropped into a hollow of the earth, isolated from thought and action. And yet some power was drawing him on, ever forward into the desolate landscape, wishing to know the end of it; or would it perhaps go on forever as it seemed to him that it might. Above him was the blue hollow of the sky, limitless, towering, empty but for a few straying birds. He gazed down at his hands, stained red with the berries, and rubbed them among the gnarled heather.

On and on, a small figure in the vast landscape, he went, half kneeling, and searching, sometimes having to jump down from peat banks as he traversed them. The ground was in many places soggy and moist, and at times his shoes sank into it as into a marsh, but mostly he moved among the tangle of heather which was dry and springy.

A voice inside was telling him, "You should go back. You don't know how long you've been away because you have no watch. What if you got lost here and no one ever found you? Your body might rot among these peat banks forever." But another voice was saying, "You've never been as far as this before. Keep on going. You might find something that you've never seen before."

And at that instant as he raised his aching back he found himself to his astonishment facing the sea. He had somehow reached the end of the moor and was standing on a promontory and there below him, it seemed for miles, was the ocean. It was a different sea from the one he knew, it looked as if no human eye before his had gazed on it. This sea had no houses near it, no boats, it seemed to have nothing at all to do with him or any other human being, it stretched as far as the eye could see in a dark endless blue. And as he looked down, trembling and amazed, he saw ducks flying far below him above the surface of the water, and, yes, surely in the distance a liner sailing slowly past. What waters, what a sea, multitudinous, glittering, like the open page of an immense blue book so that one could imagine oneself studying it, scrutinising it for its fish.

It appalled him and it exhilarated him. If he fell down there he would be ages falling, he thought, and drew back from the promontory, for his head for heights was not good. The jam jar in his hand, he stared downwards. That sea, where did it end? It seemed as if it went on forever, dancing and happy in the rays of the sun, immeasurably deep, immeasurably dangerous. All around him flew the seagulls but these were not the scavengers that followed the plough, these were the true real seagulls of a different race from the others, seagulls of the ocean, very pure, very white, with cold beady eyes staring at him as if he were an intruder into their domain.

He looked rapturously downward as if towards a treasure that had been given to him alone, an explorer of the dangerous blue waters, and as he did so he heard above him a constant humming much louder than that of an insect. When he stared upwards he saw an aeroplane moving slowly along, its wings glittering, its engine loud in the silence. He imagined the pilot sitting in his seat gazing down through his goggles at the ocean and felt for a moment a spasm of vertigo which made him draw further back.

Glancing from plane to sea and back to plane again he was overwhelmed by a sense of largeness and space such as he had never felt before. It was as if in face of the two extended blues reflecting each other the Cook, Mrs Macdonald, Mrs Murray, his mother, Kenneth, Speedy, Daial and the rest of them had disappeared from the earth, as if the whole village no longer existed, as if he had found himself in a freedom that he could hardly endure. For there was nothing here that was human, anchored to the earth, there were only stones and water and ducks and seagulls and that one aeroplane in which sat the pilot, among the clouds: he couldn't even see any sea shells for he did not dare to peer over the precipitous edge of the cliff.

He gazed down at the jam jar in his hand, at his jersey which had begun to shiver in the strong breeze blowing towards him from the sea; he looked up at the aeroplane travelling through the blue sky and then he turned away from them all and began to run into the moor where the peat banks were, where the wiry heather was growing, beyond which the village lay, with its familiar ditches and its canisters and its old shoes, and from which he could see the sea that was known to him, with the green island in the middle.

He had run for a long distance before he stopped and began to walk more decorously, only to find that in his race he had spilt many but not all of the blaeberries. When he ate the remainder they seemed to have a bitter chilly taste which he had not felt before, a sour exciting tang which made him squirm with an exquisite agonised pleasure, which scoured and cleaned his whole body.

18

"I'VE COMBED MY hair already," said Iain.

"Well, it doesn't look combed. Come here and I'll comb it for you properly."

Iain submitted himself to his mother's hands.

"And another thing. What about your shoes? Have you polished them?"

"I polished them last night."

"Let me see them. Yes, they'll do. And where's your bag?"

"I've got it."

Kenneth was still lying in bed for he was only going to the village school and didn't have to leave till later; Iain however had to catch the bus at quarter past eight for the journey to the town school. It was the 20th of August and this was going to be his first day at his new school.

He left his mother and went over to the window through which he would eventually see the red bus breasting the brae.

His mother said, "And make sure that you're polite and good mannered. Do what your teachers tell you. And look after yourself in the town. Keep away from the traffic."

"All right, Mother."

"And don't get in with bad boys. Remember that the town boys are different from the village boys. Some of them smoke and swear. Don't you learn to do that or you'll have me to answer to. Are you hearing me?"

"Yes, Mother."

Why was the bus not coming? Trembling and feverish with anticipation he waited.

"And another thing. I'm making a great sacrifice for you. I hope you'll remember that. And do well at your lessons."

It was as if she was never going to see him again and yet he would be home again that same evening at five o'clock or so.

"Sit quietly in the bus and don't play about. And no standing on the steps of the bus as I've seen other boys doing. Wait till the bus stops."

"Yes, Mother."

And Kenneth still slept open-mouthed and snoring in the bed which the two of them shared. Or at least he had been doing so when Iain had left it early on that bright and fragile autumn morning.

"Come here and I'll put your tie straight." He went over to her obediently, squirming in her hands as if afraid that she would take it into her head to kiss him, but all she did was to pat him on the head silently.

He turned back to the window and saw the bus breasting the brae. He shouted "Here's the bus, mother," and then he was running with his school bag over his shoulder to the door, hearing faintly as he passed Kenneth saying, "Good luck then." In his brown suit he ran down the path to the plank and waited there till the bus finally came. He forgot to wave to his mother who was standing at the window watching him climb the steps.

When finally the bus had started again and moved forward carrying her small son to the town she turned back to the kitchen and after a while told Kenneth roughly that it was time for him to be getting up. Today, she thought, she would do a big washing to keep her mind occupied, and after that there would be the ironing. The day would eventually pass, somehow.

"Hurry up," she shouted to Kenneth. "Are you going to lie there all day?"

As the bus was almost full the only seat Iain could find was one beside an oldish man who, he presumed, was from the next village, as he didn't know him. He sat in silence as the bus sped on, now and again stopping for passengers who were going to their daily work in the town; and he thought with trepidation of the day ahead of him.

Suddenly he heard a voice from beside him saying, "Are you going to the school then?"

He turned and saw a face with large black eyebrows and a very red nose.

"Yes," he answered shyly.

"It won't be for long now, I can tell you. It won't be for long. We will be at war soon, did you know that? According to the wireless we'll be at war. It was saying that on the wireless this morning." And the man nodded his head with great satisfaction. "Bombs and guns and aeroplanes, that's what we'll be having. Same as in the last war, only worse. Chamberlain didn't manage it after all."

Iain remained silent as he didn't know what to say. But the man didn't seem to require that Iain should speak.

"It was the trenches in the last war, but it won't be trenches in this one. It will be tanks and aeroplanes. Look what they did already in Spain. You look at it for a minute and study it but they don't teach you that in school, do they? And the boys from the villages will be off to the Navy as before, and who will look after them when they come home? They told them after the last war, Homes for Heroes, that's what they said. But they didn't give them Homes for Heroes, did they?" And his eyes glittered with malice and anger. "Did they now? I'm telling you they didn't."

A woman who was sitting in the seat behind patted the man on the shoulder and said, "Leave him alone, Rob. He's just a young boy."

"And what were they but young boys, eh? Tell me that. They

were all young boys. Huh," and he turned away from Iain, muttering unintelligibly to himself.

"Don't you listen to him," said the woman to Iain. "If it comes, it comes. You're too young to be worrying about things like that. You should be ashamed of yourself, Rob."

"All right, all right, it was just that I was in that school myself. Anyway, boy, if Macleod is still there tell him I was asking for him. Tell him Rob MacMillan was asking for him. He'll remember me. I used to be good at arithmetic. You tell him that. Rob MacMillan."

And he finally turned away leaving Iain alone, though now and again he would mutter to himself, and Iain thought that he could hear in the middle of the tirade swear-words as if the man was accusing himself of some strange wrong or sin that he had committed years ago, hating himself, bringing himself to an imaginary judgement.

When however the bus finally reached town the man suddenly shook him by the hand and said, "Good luck then, boy. And remember what I told you. Rob MacMillan is the name. You tell Macleod that Rob MacMillan was asking for him." But as Iain stepped off the bus it was as if, because of the man's words and strange behaviour, he could hear above him the hum of enemy planes and see his friends from the village setting off into a war whose meaning he could not possibly understand.

There were hundreds of them in the big hall: Iain had never seen so many boys together in the one place in his whole life. Teachers in black gowns passed up and down the aisles, looking like buzzards, wings folded. Suddenly to the lectern far ahead of him there strode a very small man whom Iain could hardly make out even by craning his neck. The small man stood behind the lectern staring unmovingly ahead of him, and the noise gradually diminished till there could only be heard the man's voice.

"This is your first day in school," said the small man in a distinct confident voice. "You will have difficulty in finding your way about at first but you'll learn as one has to learn everything in life eventually. You will be expected to be obedient and above all you will be expected to work hard. Remember, hard work is the greatest delight in life. You won't know that now but you will, you will. That's all I have to say for the moment. Good luck to you all."

The small man left the lectern and the talking began again till silenced by another, this time taller, man, who climbed the steps and told them that now they would be divided into their classes. They were to listen very carefully, for he would not repeat what he had said.

Iain, like the other boys around him, listened carefully.

It seemed to him as if all the boys in the island were gathered there.

At the interval he was standing alone in the playground when an older boy came over to him, and said, "Have you got a meek?" Iain who didn't know what a meek was looked at him in astonishment.

"A meek, a meek," the boy repeated. "You're not another of them. Do you not know what a meek is?"

"No," said Iain who was beginning to get a little frightened.

"A meek is a halfpenny."

"I haven't got any money," said Iain.

Later Iain saw some of the older boys tossing halfpennies in the air and concealing them, when they descended, on the backs of their hands, after which they would guess which sides – heads or tails – had come down: and as a result of this one or other of the two competitors would claim both coins. Meeks: so that was what they were called. Maybe some day he would learn the language of the town boys.

At lunch time he went to the house of his aunt who was staying by herself in the town, and who measured out little pats of butter on to slices of very thin bread, while she poked about at a primus stove in the half-darkness of the room. Half-blind, she would now and then clap him on the shoulder calling him a clever boy and a credit to his family, and especially to his dead father whose only surviving sister she was. A bird in a cage gazed down at him dispassionately, its head cocked on one side, while Iain ate his lukewarm pie.

"And how is your mother?" she would ask him at intervals as if she had forgotten the answer he had given her before.

"Fine," he would answer and she would say, "That's good, that's good," poking about short-sightedly with a knife or a fork.

"I don't suppose you will remember your father," she said to him at one point. "He was a fine man and he would have been very proud of you."

And she would offer him another slice of thin bread with butter on it. The room was very dark, its curtains half drawn, and there was a smell of grease and floor polish. Iain could hear the sound of traffic as it passed the house which jutted out on to the road with its low windows and its whitewashed wall.

When he had finished his food he left the house and ran all the way down to the quay where the motor boats and the drifters were lying, resting on their reflections. He walked up and down it, wishing that he could go for a sail on one of the boats, and now and again seeing a boy in wellingtons and thick white stockings swinging up the iron ladder from the depths of a drifter.

The castle in its green cloud of trees enticed him but he didn't go that day. "I am free," he thought." I can go anywhere I like except that I have to return to school at half-past one." A road which he had not yet travelled curved past the last shop that he could see, following the flow of the river which was the only barrier between himself and the castle. He imagined that the river was

swarming with trout and salmon and that across it were bridges which he would eventually cross. One day he would certainly walk among the woods which surrounded the castle, for he had never been among trees before. Nor had he ever been near a castle before, and he didn't know whether this one was inhabited or not, though it looked new with its white towers and white walls.

"'Insula, insulam, insulae, insulae, insula,'" chanted the fierce-looking man with the red almost vertical brush of hair above the intensely white face. And the class chorused the words after him.

"'Insulae – of an island or to an island', depending on whether it is the genitive or the dative you are using," said the fierce-looking man, poking with a pointer at a small hesitant boy whose name Iain did not as yet know. "Remember, boy, this is the language of the second greatest race the world has ever seen. Do you know the name of the first one?"

"The British, sir," said the boy who sat beside Iain and whose hand had shot into the air like a spring bursting from a box.

"Rubbish, boy. The British invented the steamship and the Davy lamp and no doubt the lavatory pan" – and here an extraordinary expression, compound half of mirth and distaste, crossed his face – "but they did not invent the mind. Anyone else, anyone else?" The words were shooting out of the man's mouth like bullets and his pointer thrust here and there like a sword or a spear as if he were indulging in some sort of esoteric warfare.

"The mind, the mind, boy, who invented the mind?" and the teacher poked at a fat boy who looked as if he were to cry.

The class stared at this red-haired apparition in fear and amazement. What did he mean by asking, Who invented the mind? The question didn't make sense. But the teacher, undismayed by the silence, his long nose thrust out like the beak of a ship below his hair of startling red answered his own question, emphasising the answer by banging the desk nearest to him with his pointer.

"The Greeks. The Greeks invented the mind. The Romans invented roads but the Greeks invented the mind. And don't you forget it. Some day perhaps some of you will have the privilege of learning Greek but for the moment we are concerned only with 'insula, insulam, insulae, insulae, insula'," and at the last stressed syllable he banged the desk again with his pointer as if he wished to smash it into smithereens.

"'Insula' means 'island', and remember that we are living on an island. This school we are standing on or sitting in, as is the case with some of us, is situated on an 'insula'. It is surrounded by water. If it weren't surrounded by water we would call it 'peninsula' from 'paene insula' which is the Latin for 'almost an island'. But as it is we are standing on an 'insula' that is a complete island."

And he glared fiercely at them as if daring them to deny the statement he had just made, but all they did was to sit in amazement, timorous and obedient, watching the drama being enacted in front of them, and trying to escape the lightning which writhed all round the room from the peculiar man's mind, while at that very moment though they did not know it a man who was not a Roman was pacing relentlessly up and down a room far from where they were, making plans to invade their island, sending out orders to Air Force and Navy, plotting their own overthrow and that of their mothers and fathers and sisters and brothers and the very teacher who was striding so restlessly about the room in which they were sitting. But as yet they did not know about this and were too busy evading the dramatic onslaught that was being made on them to care, an onslaught being conducted by an odd extraordinary man whose overpowering force impressed even them though they did not understand half of what he was talking about.

Later after the period was over, one of the members of the class who was repeating the first year stood outside the door of the Science Room shouting to the rest of the boys gathered around him, "They may have invented the lavatory pan but they did not invent the MIND." And they all burst out into a perfect storm of laughter which left them helpless. A lavatory pan, imagine a teacher talking about a lavatory pan!

Back in the staff room Mr Trill, for that was the name of the teacher, was stuffing tobacco into a pipe, and saying, "I saw my first year last period. I think they'll do, I think they'll do. By the time I'm finished with them they'll be all right." And he turned his attention to *The Times* and its ominous headlines. *The Times* was the only paper he bought, because he said, "You can attack *The Times* on many grounds but you can't deny that it writes sentences."

When at five o'clock the bus stopped at the path leading to his house, Iain stood for a moment gazing around him. It was as if the village had suddenly become very small and unimportant. Here there was no castle and no trees, no drifters, no motor boats, no big shops, no noise of traffic. The huddled quiet houses seemed becalmed in front of him, and the moor ancient and lifeless.

He walked up the path to where his mother was standing, waiting for him at the door. Even she had suddenly become more distant, as if she belonged to another world, where the Greeks and the Romans and the "mind" and the castle and the trees had no place. He did not wish to tell her what had happened during the day: he wanted to keep it secret. But he knew that she would ask him all sorts of questions till every morsel of his experience had been chewed and devoured. There was no sign of Kenneth anywhere: perhaps he was playing with the other boys of the village.

Clutching his new case in his hand, his case which contained his new books and his new jotters and his assignments for the following day, Iain walked up the path towards his mother who was still standing by the door shading her eyes against the glare of the sun.

19

"I'M NOT GOING to put that on," said Mrs Campbell.

"Well, we all have to," said Angus Macleod in his most officious voice. "We all have to try them on. You never know what they'll do. And the two boys will have to try them on as well."

"I wouldn't be able to breathe," said Mrs Campbell inflexibly. "Anyway they won't come as far as here."

"You never know about that. You never know when they'll come."

"I would look daft wearing that," Mrs Campbell said determinedly. "And as for the two boys they're too young."

"No, we're not," Kenneth interposed. "We're not too young." He was glad of the novelty and ready to prove that he was not frightened.

"You never know," Angus Macleod repeated. "They're beasts, animals. Have you heard what they have been doing in Belgium?" His small malicious eyes flickered at the savagery and cruelty of it. But he couldn't bring himself to tell her that they had been raping nuns, and in any case he had never seen a nun in his life. A part of him seethed happily with the idea of it.

"Well then," said Mrs Campbell, "you show us how to put them on."

He took the gas masks out of their boxes, and laid them on the table. "Perhaps Kenneth would like to try his on first," he said. "He doesn't seem to mind." And when Kenneth immediately stepped forward like a soldier on parade he fixed the gas mask to his face.

"I can't breathe," Kenneth thought, feeling the coldness of the rubber, then staring at his mother and brother and Angus Macleod through the large bulbous eyes like a fish's eyes.

He danced up and down in the room like a monster, putting his hands out to touch, first, his mother and then Iain. He was swimming in the sea, he was a fish, the room had become an ocean.

Iain stared at his masked brother, and couldn't recognise him. It was as if Kenneth had been replaced, as in a fairy story, by a complete stranger, ugly and distant and frightening, snouted like a beast.

Keep away from me, Kenneth, I don't know you, you're someone else, why are you swimming towards me like that, from the bottom of the ocean, why are you holding out your hands towards me as if to destroy me, as if you hated me? Why are your eyes glittering behind the mask?

I don't want to wear it, it's evil, I hate it.

But when Angus Macleod handed him his own gas mask he put it on, fumbling with it, till finally he had fitted it over his face. And now he and Kenneth were glaring at each other, through the bulbous eyes; and then his mother was wearing hers as well; and the three of them, masked and snouted and goggled, were watching each other, remote and cold inside their new insulated worlds. Kenneth stalked Iain about the room, while their unrecognizable mother stayed where she was, uncertain and frightened.

One was a German soldier and one was a Scottish soldier. It was a fight to the death in a country and landscape that they didn't know. They hunted each other round chairs and round the table, their disguised heads thrust out, imaginary daggers in their hands. All around them was the hissing of gas, the crackling of gunfire: the island was alive with lights and noise.

And Kenneth thought, I'll get him. He's an officer, he's left us all, he's deserted us. I'll get him. He thinks he's better than me, but he's not.

And Iain was thinking, Kenneth doesn't like me. He really wants to kill me. I'm on my own on this island, this insula, I'm an officer who's gone on a mission of his own.

Suddenly he removed his mask and shouted, "I don't like it. I don't like it." But Kenneth kept stalking him till his mother, after her mask had been removed, made him stop. She was remembering her own father, bearded and heavy, setting off for another war, his rifle strapped to his shoulder.

"Stop that at once," she shouted at Kenneth and Kenneth stopped, frightened at the violence in her voice. Slowly he removed his gas mask and laid it on the table, from which Angus Macleod took it to return it to its box.

"They're just boys," he said. "It's natural. They don't know." And he remembered his own son who would be setting off to the Navy that very week. He might never see him again, and yet not so long ago, it seemed, he had been the same age as these boys. The house would be quiet without him, he and his wife would feel the silence.

"Well," he said, "that's that. You know how to use them if you need to."

They watched through the window as he made his heavy way down the path to the road.

"Well," said their mother, "that's enough. You get on with your homework," she told Iain, "and as for you, Kenneth, you go to the well and bring me some water."

"I don't want to," Kenneth complained. "I always have to go and get the water."

"Iain has his homework to do," said his mother in an even inflexible voice. "You're not doing anything."

With a glance at his brother, Iain said that he himself would go for the water but his mother immediately checked him. "No. He's not doing anything. He has to go."

Kenneth sulkily left the room and the two of them were left alone. "You have to work hard. Remember what I'm doing for you. You'll have to become a minister or a teacher." It was as if she had already forgotten about the war and the unforeseen disasters it might bring. "I don't want you to end up with nothing after the sacrifice I'm making for you."

Iain said nothing but turned back to his books while he thought of Kenneth making his slow reluctant way to the well.

Insula, insulam, insulae, insulae, insula . . .

Of an island, to an island, from an island . . .

The teacher's head was crowned with flames and he was shouting, "Who invented the mind? Eh? Who invented the mind?" The head was burning and men in gas masks were attacking from all directions while in the far distance Kenneth was dipping the buckets into the well, his cool head bent over the cool water, far from the guns and the action.

"I don't like these gas masks," said his mother. "And who does Angus Macleod think he is? He's going about there like a sergeant major. Soon he'll be thinking that he runs the village."

Around the 'insula' the waters were bitter and salty and briny, and over them a fierce sun was shining with red vertical rays. "Kenneth will have to do more of the work now," said his mother, her head bent over a jersey which she was knitting. "You've done it long enough. I'm not standing his nonsense. I don't know how I'm going to get you a school uniform and that's for sure."

Come, Kenneth, come back from the well. Let us be as we always were, fighting and shouting at each other. I don't want to be an officer on this island. I'll help you with the water from the well.

And Iain felt a pain bitterer than he had ever known surge

through him as if for the first time in his life he was truly alone, freed of both his mother and brother, freed of the battle and the war, inside his own world of the mask and the goggles, gazing down on those other two, climbing steadily over the moor, over the sea, frightened, exhilarated, solitary: so that for a moment as he looked at his books it was as if he was still wearing his gas mask and he couldn't see them clearly.

"Yes, mother," he said.

He went back to his homework and she continued with her knitting.

NO HERO FOR THE KAISER

Rudolf Frank ISBN 0 86267 200 7

The world closed in on Jan Kubitzky on September 1914 — his fourteenth birthday. Russian soldiers, armed with guns and cannon were in the fields and similarly armed German soldiers were in the wood. Between them lay the small Polish hamlet of Kopchovka, which had been Jan's home until the day when everything in it was destroyed. When the firing stopped, only he and Flox, Vladimir the shepherd's dog, were left alive.

'*NO HERO FOR THE KAISER* is a work so remarkable that you have to wonder why it has taken so long to reach us here. The German-born author served in the 1914 war, and wrote the book from that experience. It was banned and publicly burned by Hitler in 1933. Its acclaim, we learn continues . . . Graphic, memorable . . . it's clear to see why this book was put to the flames.'

Naomi Lewis *The Observer* 1986

THE LAST HARPER

Julian Atterton   ISBN **0 86267 184 1**

This novel by Julian Atterton was shortlisted for the Young Observer Teenage Fiction Prize. Set in sixth-century Britain it tells how Gwion is forced to leave his home settlement after it is raided by sea wolves and how he finally becomes apprenticed to a master harper in the Kingdom of Rheged.

Julian Atterton is a young writer of great promise. He lives with his wife in a remote house on the North Yorkshire Moors and spends his time writing and researching into medieval history. He has studied at the Sorbonne in Paris and at the Universities of Cambridge and East Anglia. His interests include rock climbing, archaeology and acting.

THE SENTINELS

Peter Carter ISBN 0 86267 195 7

When John Spencer's parents die his uncle packs John off into the Royal Navy as a 'Gentleman Volunteer'. His ship, HMS Sentinel is bound for the worst service in the Navy, the West African Squadron, the anti-slavery patrol.

Torn by civil war and shattered by the impact of fire-power, the tribal organisation of West Africa is breaking down. One man taken as a slave is Lyapo, a farmer, captured by Dahomey warriors. Chained, desperate, separated from his wife and children, Lyapo is passed from trader to trader until he is bought by the ruthless American, Kimber, master of the slave-ship Phantom. Bound for the plantations of America, Lyapo now faces the hazards of the high seas where, when Sentinel and Phantom meet, he finds himself joining John Spencer in a desperate struggle for survival.

Winner of The Guardian Children's Fiction Award 1981.